Moments in
Between

First published in 2023 by the University of Sydney.

Funded by the University of Sydney, Faculty of Arts and Social Sciences, School of Art, Communication and English.

Sydney University Press
Fisher Library F03
University of Sydney
NSW 2006 AUSTRALIA

Email: sup.info@sydney.edu.au
sydneyuniversitypress.com.au

A catalogue record for this book is available from the National Library of Australia

ISBN: 978-1-74210-536-9 (paperback)
ISBN: 978-1-74210-537-6 (epub)
ISBN: 978-1-74210-538-3 (PDF)

Cover design: Ella Boyd and Lucie Thompson
Design and text layout: Sophie Belotti

Contents

Contents

Acknowledgements

We were searching for those small moments, the joy of the every-day, the vibrancy of passion and the shimmer of delight, and we are thrilled with how *Moments in Between* has come to life. Our theme was "simple pleasures", and we are grateful to those who made it possible.

First, and most importantly, we must thank Agata Mrva-Montoya, without whom this anthology would likely not exist. Your direction, care, and time spent with this project has been invaluable.

Thank you to Diana Reid for generously contributing the foreword for *Moments in Between*. We are honoured to have included you in this anthology.

We would like to thank all the wonderful authors and artists who submitted their work: thank you for collaborating with us as the anthology progressed through the year. Your insights and interpretations of the theme once again showcased the incredible talents of the University of Sydney's students, staff, and alumni.

To the team at Sydney University Press, thank you for your continued support for the anthology and your assistance printing and publishing *Moments in Between*.

And finally, to the anthology team: Freya, Kiya, Lucie, Kelly, Michaela, Natalie, Rose, Sophie and Vijeta. Thank you for all your hard work and the many hours you gave to the anthology this year. It's been a pleasure.

Foreword

Diana Reid

When I was younger my social aspirations were cringingly cliché: I wanted to fit in. Like most teenagers, I confused being like my friends with liking the same things as them. This meant I spent a lot of time pretending to enjoy that which gave me no pleasure. I laboured over playlists, converting each individual Youtube clip into an mp3 file and downloading the album artwork from Google Images. I used headphones to chain myself to my best friend: one earbud each, fingers in the other ear to block out the real world. I bought concert tickets and listened to the songs for weeks before so I could mouth all the words when I arrived.

It's only in adulthood that I've been able to admit that music doesn't really give me any pleasure. And I mean music in general, as an art form. Spotify is for podcasts, the radio in the car is always tuned to AM, and if I'm in a bar and someone cries "I love this song!" my usual response is to think: "Wow! There were songs playing this whole time?" I'm the aural-equivalent of the person who walks bemused through an art gallery, seeing all the pictures and reading all the little blurbs and wondering what it is that they're supposed to feel.

Such a musically defective pleasure-centre is obviously boring and regrettable. Even so, I no longer feel any shame about it, or feel compelled to hide it. That is because I have come to believe that what people find (or don't find) pleasurable reveals almost nothing about who they are.

Many people might balk at this statement – for example, anyone who has ever been excited to learn that a crush or a new friend likes the same films or books or bands. We seem to think that people who find pleasure in the same places are, in some significant way, like us – that we are *closer* to or more bonded with them for the coincidence.

But when I think of the people I love most – the people to whom I am unequivocally closest – their pleasures differ wildly from mine. Some of them lift weights for fun, or don't particularly care for movies, or would never opt for dessert. They're all pleased *for* me that I enjoy reading and writing, but that's not to say they necessarily gain any pleasure from my novels, or from novels in general.

None of this is to say that pleasure doesn't *matter*. It's just that, in our online age of constant self-analysis and representation, pleasure is delightfully irrelevant. It cannot say anything about who you are as a person because it is, fundamentally, *not about you*. On the contrary, pleasure strikes me as the experience of transcending the self.

For all the variety of pleasures rendered in this anthology, they share, without exception, this quality of transcendence. Whether it's swimming in the ocean, or eating good food, or holding a loved one's hand, or (and this was a recurring motif) listening to music – the experience of pleasure is invariably one of total *presence*. It's about subsuming your sense of self to your senses: not who you are, but what you can taste and touch and smell and see. Even in scenes of interpersonal pleasure – holding a newborn or a loved one's hand – there is still the sense that intimacy is pleasurable where it makes us part of something larger than ourselves.

Hence the glorious title of this anthology, chosen with as much care and as much credit to its creators as every other element of this project: *Moments in Between*. Pleasure is that small moment in between the resumption of a continuous, inescapable self.

And this anthology is not only a meditation on pleasure, but also an occasion for it. Reading is, of course, a paradigmatic pleasure. No matter how many and varied ways we find to *perform* reading – on social media; at writers' festivals; with the right kind of tote bag – it will always be at its heart a private act of communion between the reader and the page.

For me, the act is never more pleasurable than in those moments after I've read the last line of a great novel and I sit motionless with the book closed on my lap. Even though the story is over, there are a few precious minutes when the world it described and the feelings it evoked are more real to me than my own life. I am, in a deeply pleasurable way, not yet myself.

I am reluctant to moralise pleasure. If we accept that pleasure involves some form of escape from the self, then a life in pursuit of pleasure – hedonism – is necessarily a life that avoids responsibilities. We are, after all, the main characters in our own narratives: we have to move through time in the same body, deliberating and acting, hopefully learning from our failures, accountable to all we've done in the past. But when we think of pleasure as those moments in between – like the moments described throughout this anthology, or the moment readers will experience upon reading it – we can see that there is something fundamentally good about pleasure.

It's personal and private, but it's also universalising: we all experience it from time to time, which means we are all capable – in small moments – of being more or less than ourselves. It's in those pleasurable, egoless moments that we're particularly porous to new ideas, new feelings, new experiences. That's why when we read – properly, pleasurably, not for others but for ourselves – we can change our minds and broaden our sympathies.

The works in this anthology achieve all that and more and I thank its many brilliant authors for the pleasure.

Moments in
Between

Trains, Planes and Blackberry Pie

Freya Elizabeth Bell

Anna is already awake before her alarm sounds. It is dark and she can already hear cars in the distance, speeding along the highway that is too close to her little apartment.

The sound is constant. Dim and far away enough that she can often ignore it. Yet near enough that it is always there, even in her dreams.

It is too early for cars. It is too early to be awake. It is too early to be this tired.

Anna's eyes are shut tight as she tries to convince herself that she is, in fact, still asleep.

Sleep is comfortable. Sleep is an escape.

Sleep is . . .

Riiiiing

Where she can dream.

Riiiiing

Sleep is . . .

Riiiiing

Pointless.

Riiiiing

Anna curses the alarm and dreads what it symbolises.

Another day of drudgery.

She wonders what it would be like to wake to the sound of a rooster crowing. Or the sound of songbirds. A babbling creek, a mooing cow, a braying donkey.

She opens her eyes. Even in the fading darkness, Anna can trace the outlines of mould on the roof above her head. She watches the mould, and can almost see it growing, multiplying, spreading – it's gotten so big, so quickly. She wonders if it's worth emailing the landlord, again.

Even as she wonders about what the mould is doing to her lungs, as she breathes in, and out, and in, and out each night, she knows that it isn't worth the bother.

Steeling herself against the day, Anna swings herself out of bed. A muscle in her neck cramps and she clutches the wall in a daze of agony.

As the pain eases and the muscle relaxes, Anna glances at the eye-wateringly bright screen of her phone.

5.15 am.

She's already wasted too much time. She's going to be late.

No time for dawdling.

Straight into the shower. Out of the shower. The water is cold.

The kettle is on. The kettle has boiled.

The tea is made. The toast pops.

The tea is drunk.

The breakfast is eaten.

A handful of blackberries are snatched from the fridge.

No time to savour them.

Clothes are found and rolled for lint.

Polyester already makes her sweat.

A bag that is too heavy is hoisted onto her shoulder. Is it any wonder her neck likes to cramp?

A race to the train results in blisters that sting and ache.

An hour on a train that smells like piss. Speeding through mountains where deep bush is pockmarked by electrical lines and abandoned colliery equipment.

Anna breathes deeply. A soothing, calming breath that provides no relief, no soothing, no calming. All she smells is B.O. and urine, and a smell of something acrid and rotting.

The view from the train is depressing. Graffiti and garbage litter the tracks.

Birds peck among the rocks, hoping to find something living. Anna watches them, apathetically. A pigeon discards pieces of plastic as it looks for something to eat. Anna ignores the barb in her chest as she watches, because to feel it at all would be to feel it too much.

She wonders whether the trains scare the birds, or the rabbits, or the deer. Does the rumble rattle through their chests and into their hearts, or are they used to the terror?

Gumtrees are scarred by neon pink spray paint, marking them for execution for daring to exist so close to the train lines.

Wattles and eucalypts are suffocated by invasive ivy that should never have been here.

Anna thinks if she stood there, beside that tree, for long enough, perhaps the ivy would creep inside her. Through her mouth, or her ears, and wrap itself around her guts and strangle her from the inside out.

As the train approaches the city, the rotting bush gives way to rotting homes.

Peeling bark transforms to peeling paint.

Dead leaves transform to dead dreams.

The city smells like piss, too.

Once upon a time, Anna thought this city was magic. The Bridge and the Opera House, the winding streets, little shops, galleries and museums once brought joy and intrigue. Now it has turned to a vast cemetery, gravestones that bear down upon what was once there, in the long distant past.

In her office, Anna stares dead-eyed at her computer screen.

Meaningless data and meaningless emails eat away at her.

A manager admonishes her for missing a deadline. Because the world will stop spinning if a few million people do not see a thirty second ad for yet another chocolate bar. That is the true tragedy of a day filled with fluorescent lights, uncomfortable chairs and air conditioning that runs so cold it leaves Anna daydreaming about sunburn and heat stroke.

The only life in her vicinity is a succulent she is desperately trying to keep alive in such an inhospitable environment: a concrete cube with no windows and not a breath of fresh air, if such a thing even exists anymore.

The only wildlife is a dead moth next to her shoe.

At lunch, Anna's colleagues drink too much. Every Wednesday they have a team lunch at the pub, to "bond". The only thing the team has in common is how unhappy they are. Anna drinks a Coke that she says has rum in it. She is praised for how well she handles her liquor. She is accepted, for a minute, by the collective.

Back at the office, Anna makes a mistake on an invoice. She catches it just as her manager asks for the paperwork. The mistake is fixed before the invoice leaves her desk.

Still, she is called to a meeting where she is reminded that mistakes are not allowed. She asks when she last made a mistake such as this. The meeting ends in silence.

Anna leaves the office after dark. She can't remember the last time she finished work when it was still daylight.

She walks past offices that are devoid of human life.

No, not human *life,* she thinks. This is not life.

She walks past offices that are devoid of human activity, yet the lights remain on, as if the buildings themselves feel pressured by a constant need to prove their productivity and capitalist worth.

The train ride home is quiet.

This train does not smell quite so strongly of piss.

Anna plays music through headphones that hurt her ears.

She gazes, head resting against the glass, through grimy windows with degrading words etched into them.

A light high up in the sky catches her attention. She believes, just for a moment, that she has glimpsed a lone, distant star. But the light moves on, too quickly to be a star – a plane, taking its passengers to distant, far-off lands where people are surely happier than Anna is.

As the train moves slowly past endless suburbs, Anna closes her eyes and thinks ahead to the weekend that lies before her.

Despite the bone-deep tiredness that pervades her body, she can't help but feel buoyed by the thought of doing nothing and everything.

It'll start when she arrives home.

She throws her stiff, uncomfortable business casual clothes in the laundry hamper.

She plays her favourite playlist and stands under the burning heat of the shower, letting the water wash away the grime of a day toiling in a pointless job.

Out of the shower, Anna wraps herself in the largest, fluffiest towel she can find.

Dinner consists of tomato soup and bread. Rather simple fare, but tonight the soup is hot and sweet. The bread is soft and soaks up the soup like a sponge.

Afterwards, Anna pours apple juice into a wine glass and reclines on the sofa. Her thumb has already hit the button on the TV remote before she realises what she is doing. But of course, what else would she do on a night like this. A night when her soul needs tending to.

Cate Blanchett's voice fills the dark room and Anna relaxes just a little more. Elijah Wood reclines against a tree, and she feels as though she could float down the Anduin River or even storm the gates of Isengard with the Ents. As though she could, in fact, simply walk into Mordor.

As Gandalf dies and Frodo cries, Anna wonders why she couldn't have been born a hobbit. For most of them, the hardest thing they have to do is decide what to have for breakfast, second breakfast, elevenses, luncheon, afternoon tea, dinner and supper . . . the plight of Frodo, Sam, Merry and Pippin notwithstanding.

Afterwards, sleepy and with eyes swollen from crying at Boromir's death, Anna slips into bed.

As soon as her head hits the pillow though, she is asleep.

The next morning, she wakes before dawn. On any other day, she would bemoan this fact and beg the gods (whichever ones may be listening) to let her sleep for a little while longer.

Today, though, she lays there without worry and without longing. Her bones are tired and her muscles ache slightly. But there is nothing calling upon her today. No data, no figures, no emails, no invoices.

She lays there in a stupor until nature calls.

She stumbles through her morning constitutional, slowly coming to terms with the waking world.

This morning, instead of gulping down a mug of tea and ripping into a piece of dry toast as she contemplates her existence, Anna sets herself up on her balcony, narrow and cluttered though it is with abandoned plant containers and drying laundry.

Honey in her tea and blackberry jam on her toast, Anna watches as a kookaburra alights in the tree in her front yard. A good omen to be sure.

Anna sits there until she can no longer stand the glare of the sun and the burn on her skin.

Inside, she stands still, surveying her tiny and cluttered living room.

The floor needs vacuuming, the bookshelves need organising and everything needs dusting.

She *should* do all these things. And if she were to think beyond, to the other rooms in the flat, she *should* do the dishes and clean the bathroom and put the laundry on.

But no. Today is not a day of *shoulds*. It is a day of simple pleasures.

A day of soft music and body lotion.

A day spent reading old childhood favourites, *Anne of Green Gables* and *Winnie-the-Pooh*.

Anna scribbles in an old sketchbook. She draws wonky flowers and odd little creatures frolicking among them. She never did consider herself much of an artist. But the little world she has sketched brings her a moment of joy.

She snacks on strawberries and peppermint tea while she writes furiously in a journal. Thoughts, good and bad, tumble out of her in a wave of release.

She feels the urge to pick up her phone and check her emails. Her fingers twitch to scroll through TikTok.

She stands up and takes her phone to the bedroom. She turns it off and hides it under the mattress.

Out of sight, out of mind.

At around midday, Anna sprawls on the floor and naps in the sunshine.

There are fewer cars today. Still there, but distant, easier to ignore than usual.

Instead, as she dozes, Anna listens to the kookaburra laughing and her windchimes clinking in the breeze.

As the sun begins to set and the sky turns purple and pink and orange and blue, Anna peels herself off the floor.

She should be in pain, aching and stiff, but she feels rested and stretched out.

Tonight, it is quiet. Her neighbours are out and she's alone.

Standing barefoot at her kitchen counter, Anna's hands bring together a simple dough. Flour, water, sugar and salt. Such a simple recipe, even she can't mess it up.

In a bowl, blackberries macerate and sweeten. Anna can't help herself from scooping a finger through the berries and placing it in her mouth. Mushy and almost too sweet, she adds lemon juice, and it is perfect.

An old pie dish, rescued from an op-shop, receives the dough gently, followed by the filling.

Soon, the blackberry pie will emerge from the oven browned and bubbling. It will be too hot to eat, but that won't stop her. Her tongue will burn, and a blister will form on the roof of her mouth to match the ones on her heels.

But tomorrow, when Anna is scrubbing the toilet and dreading the week to come, she will have blackberry pie.

On Monday morning, when she needs to eat something quickly before she runs out the door, a big slice of blackberry pie will satisfy her hunger.

On Thursday night, when she comes home crying, the last piece of blackberry pie will be waiting for her.

A small thing when all you need is a small, happy thing.

A blackberry pie to satisfy you.

A Map of Ice Cream in Sydney

Zoe Morris

1. Northern Beaches

There are no ice cream shops in
the Northern Beaches –
at least not late at night in 2007
winding down black roads as the
clock ticked over and
over there – no.
This is so weird, I remember one being there
when I was a kid
in 1983.
God, we never should have promised them
they could have one.
Well, it is a beach day what do you expect?
We grab Bulla from Woolies and
eat it the next day.
It is nearly midnight when we arrive home.

2. Leichhardt

Girl, why do you always eat your ice cream so slowly,
like you're savouring every last drop?

Me, I scarf it
like a hungry dog.
And why won't you share any with us, little sister?
We're all done and you
you've still got more than half.
It was your decision to eat it quick.
Well, mine tasted disgusting anyway,
like cold medicine.

3. Ashfield

Neopolitan
has always been one of my favourite flavours.
Our pastor scoops horizontally across the pink, white, brown
for all the kids waiting in line
with plastic bowls.
I don't understand
why some children insist on
mixing up all the colours until they become sludge.
These people don't understand
variety and distinctness.
I have always been a connoisseur,
a hedonist who knows
what she wants.

4. Croydon Park

I always get scared of
the fucking mural
on the front of the ice cream shop.

The people look real for just a second
and I think
who brought this
delightful 1950s nuclear family to 2016
to eat gelato in Croydon Park?
But their faces are too smooth
and they smile too much
to be real.
Oh well, they can still sit
next to my netball team,
we're celebrating a good season.
I eat my mango gelato slightly shamefully.
It was no thanks to me,
I suck.

5. Campsie

We forget to buy spoons
so I scoop it out of the tub with my fingers
like I'm digging for something.
You laugh at me.
This was back when we walked down the suburbs in dry heat;
I think of you when the smell of the season changes.
Who knows what you want
when you're seventeen.

6. Circular Quay

Double scoop: strawberry and mango.
Boy said I looked pretty,

holding it in my hand.
He didn't know he was my first kiss.

7. Belmore

My friend says her flavour
tastes like nostalgia, like her favourite book.
Light yellow with rainbow sprinkles.
My flavour is "Cheesecake",
with raspberries swirling
in creamy vanilla.
Maybe in five years, when we're all grown up, it'll taste
like nostalgia too.

8. Newtown

Did you know ice cream could be sticky?
I didn't.
Not sticky like lemonade left on clammy hands
but sticky like
saltwater taffy.
We gulp Turkish coffee,
tiny silver cups
of fire
on light days sweet as Turkish Delight.

9. Auburn

We meet up 9 am on Monday,
because our respective adult calendars

are unreasonable.
I peel off the plastic wrapper
like cracking the most precious
little green egg –
it is round, buoyant,
gorgeous, hold it with your hand
and kill it softly with your mouth.
Mochi ice cream,
best served
where cherry blossom trees weep pink petals.
August is for heartbreak.

Holding Hands

Juan Pablo Guevara Morales

I want to tell you that I am here
without voicing it,
I want to let you know that I love you
without saying it
I want to hold you
without smothering you.

All these things I want to do,
somehow, someway,
this all happens, when I hold your hand.

A Morning of Bliss

Ashleigh Cuthill

I hear a snuffle – and I am instantly awake, curled protectively around the little body currently trying to bury itself into my shoulder. Peering through the dark, I glance at the clock, and start to pat the little bottom, wriggling now, to induce the extra sleep that's required at this early hour. Replacing his dummy, I rock him gently and feel it in his movements as he drifts back into slumber. A little peck on his brow and – there – he is fully relaxed. I close my own eyes, preparing to doze until it is time to rise and face the day. The warm body in front of me fits perfectly into my chest, his feet resting on my thighs. He smells like milk and baby wash; soft, pure smells that define infancy. Slowly time passes, and the light inside the room grows ever stronger.

My thoughts drift, and I distantly hear the soft catch of the baby gate that signals the arrival of another warm body. By the lack of accompanying fanfare, I can tell that more snuggles are in store this morning. I half roll over and am rewarded with the presence of my still half-asleep daughter lifting the covers and climbing into my bed and arms before settling down among the pillows. Shifting, I lie on my back and cuddle my youngest children, amazed and a little despondent at how quickly one grows into the other. At three years old, my daughter still enjoys a morning snuggle – often joining me in bed in the darkest hours before dawn, seeking warmth and comfort after facing the night on her own.

In the blink of an eye, she will no longer need this ritual. I squeeze a little tighter in a fruitless effort to ward off that day. Their presence beside me is a comfort, it lets me know they are safe and well, and my arms around them tells them they are loved.

Completely awake now, I listen for the presence of my eldest child above the silence of the house. Closer to five years old, it is only when sleeping that he resembles his infant self. He has long since lost the elements of toddlerhood and is gaining ever more markers that signify boyhood. As always, he sleeps soundly and wakes rapidly – he has never needed a gentle start to the morning to keep an even temperament. As an infant he was eager to seize the day and this trait shows no sign of disappearing. I wonder what a teenage version will be like?

Like the dulcet ring of a gong, I can hear the moment his eyes open and with an excited gasp, there's a scramble, a loud clinking of the gate and a tumble of feet. He appears in the doorframe, eager to share his excitement for a new day. Is it swimming lessons or gymnastics, do I have preschool or day-care? Is it a home day today? Every option has its perks and there is no bad one; they are only a way to mark the rising and falling of the sun in their blessed and lucky youth.

"Good morning, Alex," I say. "Did you sleep well?"

He has brought a book with him, and this morning we are going to learn to count with *Thomas the Tank Engine*. With very few words, the book is a perfect choice; he knows all the engines by now, and can recite it by heart – he is on the cusp of reading himself. I have noticed him choosing these simpler books again as his understanding of what reading is grows. I have always fostered a love of reading in the kids and actively encouraged books in bed; it's an easy way to wake up – I am a slow riser and relish the opportunity of a few more minutes in bed as well. This little morning ritual satiates their need for entertainment from the get-go: we can go exploring from the comfort of a cosy bed. I shuffle over and invite him in too, Ivy stirs and groans, also a slow riser, and we all snuggle down together.

As I read the book, Robbie becomes more animated, straining to reach the pages and share in his part of the counting. So, I prop him up to see better and once we have counted to ten, there is another shuffle around. Alex, who by now is more restless and fidgety, ends up cross-legged with the book and stares at the page with the engines and their names and numbers. He starts to point to his sister and "test" her on them, a game we played with him when he was younger. "Who is number seven?" Toby, of course, an easy one as he is the favourite. "What is special about Douglas and Donald?" They're twins! Not such a foreign concept in our family where Mama and Daddy are both twins themselves. My two eldest are engaged with their conversation and Robbie is eager to not be left out. I undo his sleeping bag and prop him up over my legs to watch. While not yet able to crawl, he wriggles and squirms, so determined to make his way over to the book. Reaching them, he lifts onto his arms and stares avidly at the bright pages, fascinated by what he sees. Noticing his interest, Alex starts to teach him the engines as well; no doubt, in a blink of an eye, Robbie will be participating in the conversation too.

It is a happy scene, a peaceful one. Not always guaranteed in the mornings when people wake tired and hungry, and I embrace the beauty of it, the pleasure it brings. Robbie is grunting now, trying to eat the book as five-month-old babies do, and Ivy attempts to keep him away, while Alex subtly moves the book out of reach. Sensing the end of harmony, I announce it's time for breakfast, and Alex and Ivy race off down the corridor. Robbie rolls over, watching them go, biding his time until he too can join them. And it's over. The older two are making noises in the kitchen that are hard to attribute to any helpful act. I sigh contentedly and kick off the covers, picking Robbie up to head out there and join them. Already the realities of the day are focusing my mind as the simplicity of the moment fades gently away. It is now a memory; one I can recall when the busyness of life threatens to take over.

The Heater

Juan Pablo Guevara Morales

Cold fingers tentatively stretch out,
painful bones and dry skin. Then,

sweet tingle of heat,
blood rushing from head to feet;
a singular kiss of relief. Warmth
the frosty wind outside,

static and paralysed in the hot comfort
of a humble heater,
a simple pleasure.

Carlton Crescent Summer Hill

Zoe Morris

Carlton Crescent juts out from the highway
like a small twig from a big trunk
and it's next to the railway
so when the sky softens
the train traffic lights
emerge like green stars.
There is a small shop,
on the corner of Carlton and Prospect Rd –
it sells dolls and I never see it open.
In 1908, a greengrocer used to live there, did you know that?
If you walk down far enough
you can see the park, Darrell Jackson Gardens
named after the longest serving alderman in Ashfield
(an alderman is a member of council).
The grass is green and lush. He died in 1997
and when I had my eighth birthday party there in 2011,
I wished my friends a happy birthday back
even though it wasn't their birthday at all.
I wonder if the grass remembers us.
If you walk down further you will see the Summer Hill Hotel.
When the light is getting dark

you can see warm lights,
shining like tiny suns
the colour of goldfish,
people sitting on the terrace, their voices a warm buzz.
The smell of beer hits your nose
as you walk past the open door.
In my experience,
if you walk any further
down Carlton Crescent
you will not be home for at least an hour
and your mum won't understand
why you're out so late.
You can follow the street
all the way down to Lewisham Station,
pressing close to the metal railway fence
like a man and his dog.
The streets will get darker then,
and quiet,
and mosquitoes will
probably nip your legs.
Or you can just turn around then,
make your way back to the highway,
which is lit up like an arcade machine,
pressing the dirt into the white footpath,
the same path you've trod a thousand times before.

In the Key of

Atticus Santamaria

I'm about two years old and my family and I are attending the wedding of some random relative (I have a big family, it's easy to lose track). The band is playing, and there I am, standing on my highchair, conducting them.

Precious, isn't it?

So began my love affair with music. I have eclectic taste. I'm a bit rock and roll. I'm a bit country. I'm a bit classical, opera, blues, jazz, pop, hip-hop, metal . . . well, you see my point.

Music is intertwined with my clearest memories. Being six years old on Sunday afternoons, those hated Sunday afternoons. School starting the next day and being all too aware of the limited amount of freedom I had left. Even so, the unpleasantness was mitigated by music. I remember the golden light pouring through the lounge room window as I listened to Mum's copy of *Teaser and the Firecat* by Cat Stevens through the record player. Picking up the needle and placing it exactly where "Moonshadow" started on the LP.

Yes, I am old enough to have listened to records. Ask your grandparents what that was like.

Trips to and from school in beat-up cars; the only things working consistently in any of them? The radios. Mum preferring to listen to cassettes of Peter, Paul and Mary, and Donovan. Singing along until my older brother told me in no uncertain terms to shut up. To this day, may the gods help me, I still know all the lyrics to "I Love My Shirt".

Yes, there really is a song called that.

Afternoons spent with Mum in the kitchen, listening to *Rumours* by Fleetwood Mac, also on cassette, watching her as she cooked.

Ask your parents what cassettes were like.

I remember being excited when my parents finally scrounged up enough money to buy a CD player, knowing that there was now a whole new world open to me. Buying my first CD to play on it: a cast recording of *Joseph and the Amazing Technicolour Dreamcoat* because we were studying it at school. Falling asleep on the living room couch as I listened to it on repeat. We didn't have much when I was a child, but there was always music, and over the years the love affair only became more passionate.

Listening to The Cranberries and The Smashing Pumpkins in Year 7 English, two of my teacher's favourite bands, and being so carried away that I wouldn't do my work. I remember the first time I heard "Down Again" by The Superjesus and being blown away, developing, I'm slightly embarrassed to say, a massive crush on the lead singer. During the HSC, I listened to "Clint Eastwood" by Gorillaz non-stop as I studied, the lyrics fitting the situation perfectly. That year, after the stress of exams was over, I went to my first music festival with a friend and saw TISM with their hilariously filthy stage show. Throughout my childhood, adolescence, young adulthood and now (almost) middle age, there has been music.

But there's more to my love of music than simple enjoyment. Music is the reason I'm still here.

When I was eleven or thereabouts, I developed a severe mental illness. Psychosis had me in its grip and I believed other people could read my thoughts. That my thoughts were so strong they were leaking out of my ears. That wasn't the worst of it, but I won't go into further detail.

Music was my saviour.

To have some privacy, I would listen to music. My Discman's earphones would rarely leave my ears. Music would, or so I believed, block my thoughts from escaping and give me some pleasure as a bonus. Music kept me safe at a time when I had never felt more alone, kept me in touch with reality when I was struggling to hold on to it.

I don't believe such things anymore, but music is still my companion in survival. I use music now to regulate my emotions. To help focus. To explain how I'm thinking and feeling when I don't have words of my own. It connects me to others and the world and grounds me. And, of course, I listen to music just because I love it.

Though perhaps "love" isn't the right word for how I feel about music. It's a part of who I am. My heartbeat. Constant. A pleasure that I will cherish for the rest of my life.

Anthem for the Fryless Dystopian

Joel Fitzgibbons

I forgot the dream
That I had last night
Because I awoke
To a dreadful sight:

The news, it did seem
Completely unright.
Like midnight creatures,
It gave me a fright.

The message appeared,
The light burnt my eyes,
The news informed me:
"We're all out of fries."

"This can't be!" I screamed,
Though tears filled my eyes.
I scrambled to see:
Had I been fed lies?!?

It took a few tries
To unlock my phone.
Typing much faster
Than any has known.

"The making of chips,
We have indeed ceased,"
Said the man in charge.
My terror increased.

"Protest, you can try,
We have more power."
My phone it then dropped;
I start to cower.

What am I to do
In such a fresh hell?
Illegal French fries,
Should I start to sell?

Wind up in a cell?
Never to be freed?
That would not do well.
My pants: they were peed.

Just then I noticed
I lay on my side.
I had just been up!
All logic defied.

Had that been the dream
I thought discarded?
Perhaps! But my fear
I still regarded.

I reached for my phone
And what did I see?
French fries permitted.
And to that, *oui oui.*

Brown Girls and White Dreams

Sharmila Jayasinghe

Maya wasn't at an age for pretend play, but as she watched *Kabhi Khushi Kabhie Gham* with her mother, she pretended she was Rahul Raichand, the golden boy, and her mother, Nandini Raichand, his devoted mother.

The fantasy filled Maya's heart. Maya didn't enjoy watching Hindi movies, but she cherished the shared moments of closeness with her mother. The pair tapped their toes to the tune pounding through the speakers and munched on deep-fried sugar-coated breadfruit, while Maya's grandma sat on a low ottoman and sang lyrics she didn't understand. It was a perfect moment.

The bond broke when her brother intruded. Mixing avocado, powdered milk and sugar in a bowl, he plopped down between her and her mother.

Maya grunted. "Ammaaaa," she protested, seeking an intervention. Her mother tousled her brother's head of spirals and ordered Maya to move so that his bum could fit in well. He made fun of what was happening on the screen, ravenously devouring the avocado concoction, blissfully unaware his male status had trumped over her femaleness yet again.

"No wonder girls want to be boys," Maya muttered. She was not angry for long. The emotion appeared like dew on grass; one minute it was there, the next minute gone.

Maya pulled herself off the couch and settled on the floor between her grandma's legs. As if on cue, the old woman started running her fingers through Maya's hair, attempting to tame the unruly curls.

Maya sighed, holding in a bit of the air so as not to fully deflate. She'd been four when her mother brought Jeremy home. He was wrapped tight like an Egyptian mummy Maya had seen in the touring Tutankhamun exhibition. Maya had watched the wrappings come off to reveal a small figure, white and skinny like a starved chicken. Jeremy had grown up to be a beautiful young man with porcelain skin. His eyes were the colour of dirty rainwater. They stood out against his dark curls and made him look exotic. Maya loved her brother, but she couldn't help notice the difference in the affection they were served. On occasions when it was undeniable, her escape was to her grandmother.

The old woman surprisingly favoured the girl over the boy. "කැරපොත්තු බර්ගර්," the old woman teased the boy when her son-in-law wasn't present. "Cockroach Burgher," she called him with no reservations. Her grandmother would continue: "Colour no good, name no good."

"But you," she would say, lathering "Fair and Lovely" on Maya's face, "you have perfect tan colour. Easy to attract good Kandy boy."

For the old grandma, marriage was a girl's way to liberation; to do what she couldn't do under her father's roof.

But marriage had to be done right. She believed Maya could right the wrong of her own daughter, Maya's mother, who ran away with a man who was not of the same caste and who certainly was not a good "Kandy boy".

"Good Kandy boy can change your Lansi name back to good Kandyan surname," Maya's grandma often said. The old woman genuinely believed Maya had that power.

Maya failed to understand the hype about Kandyan names and Kandyan boys.

She had been to Kandy only once in her life. It had been the year her parents decided to visit their homeland and face all the relatives they were avoiding. They had landed in the heat and dust of Colombo midday on an April afternoon – "the worst time to take the kids home," those who knew had warned Maya's mother and father, but they had not listened. "They are Sri Lankan kids. They will be alright."

Maya had made up her mind that she hated the country before she'd even boarded the plane at Kingsford Smith. The trip made her miss Melissa's birthday party, one to which only popular girls were invited. Maya wasn't popular, but an invite had fallen on her lap nevertheless.

"There will be other birthday parties," her mother had assured. Maya doubted there would be.

From the Colombo airport, it had taken six long hours in a not-so-comfortable train for them to reach Kandy. Her parents had argued the whole way.

"This is too much, Priya, look at them, they are exhausted." Maya's father had been concerned about the children's wellbeing. "We should have planned to stay at Mum's for a couple of days."

Maya's mother wouldn't hear of it. "*Amma* and *loku aiya* know we are landing today. We can't dilly-dally without going to see them straight away," she had said. "I have disappointed them enough," she added, paving the way to a bigger argument that had lasted until they got into a rusty old Benz waiting for them at the train station in Kandy.

Kandy was not like the place in the tales of castles, kings, kingdoms and jewels she had heard. It was hot, humid and full of mosquitos. The sea of people, buildings and vehicles almost bumping against each other shocked Maya. Her grandma's house was a far cry from the old government house in the middle of Parramatta Park that Maya had always imagined as a model: old, with a newness about it. Grandma's house most certainly was old, ancient even, but without any newness. The lights at night were dim inside as if the wires couldn't carry electricity that far into the middle of nowhere. Maya hated the "Pinol" smell that emanated from the toilet that had been put in specially for them. She hated squatting on the floor to do her business even more.

But she did catch the eye of a great many Kandy boys. She was thirteen, fresh from her puberty celebrations and blossoming into a young woman. The boys she met thought her exotic. They paid attention and called her *suddhi* just because she lived in a foreign land. Maya's little heart skipped a beat every time someone lingered over her. If she was honest, Maya would have admitted that her first experience of love happened in Kandy. She'd been close to kissing a boy behind the corrugated iron shed at the back of the house when her mother caught her. She had made quite a stir then. Her mother had been furious she was canoodling with the servant's son. Maya learnt then there was a pecking order, difference in caste, religion and what-not, and there were boundaries she should never cross. Her mother didn't let her forget, not even when they returned home.

"Friendship is one thing, marriage is another," her mother had preached, filtering Maya's group of friends and approving only the ones with names she could recognise. Maya could have argued if she wanted to. After all her father was a Bartholomeusz, with a Dutch heritage her mother's family had not considered a good match. But Maya didn't oppose, she was not brought up to fight.

While Maya's mother filtered her friends, her grandmother took every opportunity to find her a good match.

"Boy like him. Sweet boy, no?" Maya's grandma admired the hunk prancing around on the screen.

Maya laughed amused. "Shah Rukh Khan?"

"Sweet boy *ne*. Sure good husband! For you marry, we find boy like that. Good Kandyan, good dancing boy."

Maya's mother lost interest in the rain-drenched dance on screen the moment she heard marriage being discussed. Her children were at that age. Letting the on-screen couple dance on mute, she turned her head towards the conversation.

"Find me a good Kandyan wife too," Jeremy said. Having finished with his sweet avocado, he licked the spoon.

"The leggy brunette?" Maya asked. She was not really causing trouble. It was no secret that her brother was seeing a girl said to be "model material", with thick dark hair and botoxed lips.

"Nah. She is a dream chaser. Wants a career and traveling the world and all that bullshit," he complained. "Brown girls are the best wife material."

Maya pressed her lips tight so that her own dreams and desires wouldn't fly out. To speak them wouldn't get her anywhere. Her brother was just like her father. They felt a girl's worth was in being a good mother and a good wife. Their opinions were set in stone. Changing them was like squeezing water off sand.

"How are we going to find all these Kandyans?" Maya asked, just for light banter.

"Many cousins in Kandy," Grandma said, still combing her hands through Maya's curls.

"Eeww, that's horrible, *Aththamma*. I can't marry a cousin."

"Why *eeww*?" Maya's grandmother asked. "I marry cousin. So many years happy." The old woman pulled her hands from her granddaughter's hair, annoyed her marriage could be condemned by that ugly sound: *eeww*.

Be Still

Caitlin Anderson

17 March 2022

I happened upon an unexpected disappointment in the recesses of my brain this evening. I'd run my usual five-kilometre route up and down Pittwater Road and finished up in front of the Surf Life Saving club with the intention of catching the final moments of the sunset. Autumn sunsets are superior in my opinion. Cool pinks, soft orange, rainbow paddle pop blue, all seemingly dulled and yet made crisp as the sun's warmth withdraws and the cool evening air floods in.

Perched on the sandstone wall, I attempted to cool down after the run, half-heartedly remembering to stretch my calves, which will eternally cause me grief due to my (and arguably much of the population's) incapacity to abide by physiotherapists' prescriptions of thrice daily stretching and strengthening routines. The stage was set and primed for my enjoyment: a slowing heart rate, cool wind refreshing the warm dampness of my arms, the appearance of one of my heart's delights – a peppy schnauzer waddling by – alongside the local iguanas (retirees) that populate Collaroy's ocean rockpool.

I waited. Perhaps I was expecting a feeling of overwhelming peace, or the steadiness of contentment, or the delight in simplicity, or the childlike awe in sitting before the cosmic process of an ancient event universally witnessed. Perhaps I was hopeful that the beauty I could intellectually comprehend in the incredible process of "Rayleigh scattering" that determines the yellows, oranges and reds of a sunset would seep into my heart and soul and lead me to feel joy. The sun had set, the smattering of onlookers was dispersing, and I waited. My heart felt numb, darkness filled the sky and I walked home.

I'd followed Julia Baird's instructions from *Phosphorescence* that provide guidance on how to experience wonder: I had stopped, I had noticed, I had attended to a wonderful phenomenon that, for the majority of our lives, we irregularly acknowledge. I had attempted the homework correctly with insufficient results. My diagnosis? A cognitive block. Simple pleasures aren't so simply pleasurable when daily life is an intensified reminder of trying circumstances.

October 2020 to April 2022 was a snowball of troubles: I watched our last living cavalier deteriorate and she died in my arms; my family sold our childhood home; I moved to the Northern Beaches to live with my godparents, which, while beautiful, distanced me from my church community, work and family; and my best friend broke up with me, after a two-year-long relationship.

I've since yo-yoed through the upper and lower passageways of the window of tolerance. From hyper-arousal in the form of energy-leaching anxiety, over-exercising and sleeplessness, to hypo-arousal in the form of numb depression and relational withdrawal. After confronting the sleeping beast of insecurity that had been lying dormant for the two years I'd received affirmation and affection from a partner, I am now in a state of limbo, wondering why everyone else seems to be getting on with their lives while it feels like I've been pushed out of the car. On a seemingly barren highway, I'm at a point of wondering what to do next. It may appear as if I'm out the other end and reminiscing on being in the valley and making it through to the mountains, but I'm still very much trying to come to terms with being on my lonesome again.

Mountain and valley metaphors are helpful in this arena. It's felt like I'm on a steep path but it's at an incline that requires big, confident steps. I naively thought I could navigate it by traversing the slope sideways with the hope that I'd eventually find myself moving upwards along the path. Much to my chagrin, after avoiding and despairing, accepting and mourning, I had become this angry, envious and bitter boulder that was gaining momentum; momentum that might find me hurtling down the slope, letting splinters fly from my angry heart into those around me.

The breakup maxim is accurate – there's no handbook or recipe for going through this kind of emotional recalibration. Instead, what I do have control over are daily choices, and there are a ridiculous number of choices to make in a day when one is hyper aware of themselves and others, accompanied by the feeling of helplessness amidst circumstances.

I was wanting a quick fix: I wanted to feel the nourishment and tranquillity that comes with a still mind, a grateful heart and a joyful spirit. But, like the cultivation of a garden, time, care and integrity were tools I needed to learn how to use again so that I might, in a new way, discover and appreciate life's smaller gifts.

And how best do we learn? By following the example of others. I'm curious what the colours are in others' lives, the threads in the tapestry, the motifs in the music of life. What follows are observations of my life's orbiting planets (people) and their simple pleasures. The hope being that I might plug into their hardwire of what it's like to cultivate and cherish moments and things so that someday soon I, too, may know where to find such peace.

3 May 2022

A sad irony I begrudgingly admitted in early May concerned my fraudulent research. Don't be alarmed, I'm not guilty of plagiarism or the like. This is a case of integrity and lack of it. My doctorate research explores the literary representations of encounters between humanity and ecology in climate change fiction. Or, more simply, my research asks, why, when human characters encounter nature, do authors focus on the algorithm "nature + awe = humility"?

In the past three months, I can think of two occasions when, in the presence of nature, I experienced awe and wonder. Even then, what I experienced felt lacklustre and almost superficial. My movement in and out of the window of tolerance has worked in me an off-kilter manner of relating to the world and to others. In late March, my psychologist advised that I seek out self-soothing comforts to cope with my emotional instability. Unfortunately, for much of the past two months, such comforts have involved self-preservation methods and superficially soothing activities. I took the liberty of subconsciously convincing myself that TikTok, online shopping and self-centred forms of relating to friends and family (complaint, moping) were going to be the balm to my broken heart.

Thankfully, literature, podcasts and loved ones have tugged at the rope that anchors me to this world and I've been reminded of what I believe humans crave most and require to survive: ecological exposure – soothing, shocking, nourishing moments of stillness and activity in nature.

While listening to a brilliant podcast series by Elizabeth Oldfield called *The Sacred* and reflecting on episodes involving interviews with Rupert Read, Stuart Ritchie and Frank Cottrell-Boyce, I moulded my own identification of what I believe to be sacred: simple pleasures seen in nature and in people. We are sensory beings and there is much to wonder at: beauty, taste, sound, colour, the scent of sea air, the cackle of wild, carefree laughter.

Humans have this strange ability to get used to things. To get used to smells and sounds and sights, to circumstances once shocking, abrasive and painful, and which carry the imprint of pain but are now bearable. I've been fortunate enough to live by the ocean for the past seven months and it's been two months since I've sat on the shore and watched the ocean. Isn't that sad?

On a drive home from work listening to my audiobook, I was reminded to seek out nature and soak in the very experience I write about – encounters with the natural world. I went for my afternoon run with the intention to stop and sit for a time as the sun set. And what did I do? I stretched, sat for a minute looking at the pink clouds, and immediately walked home.

What went wrong? It felt like I'd forgotten how to be still, like I'd forgotten how to receive and enjoy, after months of yo-yoing between the hyper and the hypo – the anxious busyness and apathetic numbness. Disappointed at my subconscious apprehension to be still and enjoy the sunset, I returned to *Phosphorescence* where the concept of meditation intrigued me. Baird writes about the occupation of space, and I realised that I had made myself so large in my own emotional universe. I needed perspective to remember that it can be good to feel small – Baird would argue that it quietens a frenetic soul.

How uncomfortably accurate. My self-prescription? Cultivate awe. Daily. And discover again the things that heighten my awareness of the world and of others, that might diminish my self-interest and self-consciousness. Observe others, notice them, and notice my own habits, as well as seek out opportunities to immerse myself in a moment. Notice the senses. Though I would have to find alternatives to Baird's remedy of ocean swimming because the big blue is sadly not an environment I find calming (much to the chagrin of my family).

11 May 2022

My homework was as follows:

1. When making morning coffee, drink slowly. Give the drink *space*. Enjoy it as a singular activity without multitasking.
2. Protect work time. Minimise distraction and try to focus and tick things off from the list. Why is this in the cultivating awe list? Because for me, to best prepare myself to enjoy something, I know that I'd prefer my to-do list to be taken care of.
3. Go for a walk and sit in front of the ocean. Enjoy the sun for as long as possible, even if it's only for ten minutes. Just sit, be still and enjoy the gift.
4. When dressing to go out – choose clothes and jewellery that will make you feel good. Not out of vanity but in the style of enjoying a gift. There can be a posture of gratitude and enjoyment here.
5. When having dinner with friends and family, listen, share, enjoy the food prepared for you or by you. Taste and savour. Store away the memory.

13 May 2022

Life has hurtled by this week, and I didn't step off the tracks to be slow and relish things. I drank my coffee fast, I wolfed down food, I went for runs, and when I became bored or tired, I scrolled on my phone. I screenshotted a tweet that referred to "slowmaxxing": reading long, fat books and "making forty-eight-hour chocolate chip cookies" with the instruction:

> You need to spend hours watching wildlife, you need to spend 15+ mins making your coffee. You need to

breathe in and breathe out. You need to be slowwwwwwwwww (yes, ten Ws).

Goodness me, it takes a lot of effort to be present, but I guess, like all projects of habit and ritual, discipline, focus and intention are required.

The reality is that since March, I've wanted to be in the future, six months at least, five years at most, with pain and memories behind me, enjoying the things I'm preparing for. The least original revelation I keep bumping into is that when disruption to normality occurs, and when one must rebuild a sense of self, slowly attending to daily habits, routines and opinions are necessary in order to prepare for the slip back into purposeful, energetic living.

I want daily simple pleasures. Desperately. I want to protect them but first I must establish them. I want simple pleasures embedded in my memory and being, that shape my character and outlook on life. I'm at a point in the journey of grief where the valley is sloping upwards and the sky looks a little brighter, but there are still moments where I am rudely alerted to what has been lost. Simple pleasures may be the balm to those sharp "lemon juice in the papercut" moments, or more appropriately, "hand sanitiser in the papercut" moments.

Am I trying too hard though? Can one seek out simple pleasures so desperately that they lose their very simplicity? That may be so, but at the very least, I want to learn curiosity again, to learn wonder.

Another diagnosis: I'd forgotten or repressed the capacity to be in a childlike state of wonder. The beauty of simple pleasures is that they are unique to each person, where I hope this piece of writing may suspend judgement and rather attend to little human idiosyncrasies that expose our full humanity – that in the midst of dark times, pain and real tragedy, sparks of wonder manifest, where life's legitimate complexities are briefly overshadowed by life's extraordinary simplicities.

17 May 2022

A short list of simple pleasures observed:

1. Jenni's passionfruit vine. She keeps a record each year of how many fall. On Wednesday morning, I informed her that another had fallen and she gleefully cheered and rushed to log the latest addition into her spreadsheet.
2. Ally's enjoyment of opening windows in her Newtown apartment to create a cross-breeze. She can hear the trains, and she likes to know that the world around her is moving. She is a part of its living tapestry.
3. Ben's evening of cooking, a walk, Greek yoghurt, scented candles and a hot shower. A soothing recipe of self-care to prepare oneself to go back out into the world and continue the daily work of caring for others.
4. The North Household is a cosy haven where homemade granola, prayer, dandy chai and fresh bread are constant companions. Georgia and Ben are delighted by the preservation of food. Nothing goes to waste under Georgia's watchful eyes – teabags, paper plates, stale bread, sour milk, wrinkled vegetables, fallen flowers – all are precious in her sight. Sour milk will be transformed

into yogurt and old veggies will be transformed into five kilograms of salsa. Salsa that must be *burped* . . .

A list of simple pleasures happened upon by chance, perhaps by lending my mind to a posture of openness.

1. Snorkelling – the bright blue and bright yellow on the bellies of fish, and pink coral that looks like a giant brain.
2. Morning cup of hot coffee – routine, comfort. It's instant coffee and it's delectable.
3. Panda the Pomeranian and Cricket the Boxer – the innocence and energy of dogs.
4. The YouTube series displaying Matilda Goad's London apartment. It reminded me of the *Paddington* films, which I adore (and which are sadly linked with painful memories of a past life). It was soothing to see someone care deeply about something, to see someone's passion for design and beauty.
5. Music. Groovy music. During dinner with a friend, he pushed me to remember that I'm passionate about music. I love the saxophone lines in Masego songs, I like the orchestral versions of Josh Pyke songs. I cringe at music being one of my simple pleasures but that feels a little arrogant. I like to listen to music according to season and location. How versatile and experimental a medium to enjoy and share with others.

By noticing, by attending to niche and personal human experiences, daily life becomes interspersed with moments of loveliness, joy, beauty, passion and fun. Something so precious has been to witness what people are passionate about. It's contagious and I want to catch others' joy. What better way to proceed through many stretches of busyness, of bleakness, sadness and the mundane than with moments that brighten and augment life.

20 May 2022

We must slowmax. We must be still. We must retreat. We must boldly advance. We must look, see, smell, taste, touch, laugh, cry, scream. The world went dark for me for a time and while I'm not on the other side yet and not in a state where I can reflect on the stark contrast from before to after, I am in the healing territory, where I'm bumbling about, getting many things wrong and learning what helps.

And what helps? A good song (James Taylor, Lizzo, Cory Wong), the Hamish and Andy podcast, a friend to make you laugh at her surprisingly serious fear of cockroaches, an autumn sunset of golden orange and cool pink, hand-picked blood orange grapefruits, and an apple crumble with cheap vanilla ice cream. Those have been my simple pleasures so far.

21 May 2022

But what about when I'm sad? When I'm anxious? When I feel unsettled and choiceless in this "new normal", when all that's happened in the past few months and the many changes to come suddenly slam the breaks and whiplash causes my heart to jerk? It's the end of May and I'm scared. Things aren't simple, and I've been trying to adjust to new friendships, circumstances, routines and the like. But my heart is still tender, I still miss "him", I'm tired and I wish things were how they were six months ago. Where do I go with that?

Sweetness seems inaccessible, loved ones feel far away, I can't recall the last time I laughed heartily. I'm scared of time with myself, I'm scared of the present and future, and lamenting the past. Where is pleasure? Where do I look for joy? What can I indulge in, reflect upon and cherish so that my brain and heart might practice gratitude and feel peace? What am I looking forward to?

I've just seen a social media update from old mate/ex that hurt me more than I thought it would. So here we are, 7.07 pm on a Thursday night and uncertainty is a cold shadow leeching warmth from my soul. This all sounds quite bleak and dire. I'm definitely overtired.

23 May 2022

The 2022 Sydney Writers Festival was a catalogue of simple pleasures. Rebecca Solnit and Julian Barnes passed on a few precious gems of truth. We need persuasion and inspiration. We need bread and roses.

1 June 2022

I spent the last weekend of May in Leura with one of my oldest friends, Clare.

Clare is a powerhouse, a whirlwind – energetic, reliable, direct, curious and a woman of passion. She's unashamedly herself and in times of laughter, dancing, quiet and sadness, she is magnetic – her love for life and others overflows. Clare is also ruthless – relationships and circumstances have their natural lifecycle but Clare is one to readily evaluate and adjust in order to protect herself and ensure that her paragons of authenticity and motivation are prioritised.

Where does this weekend away fit into my search for simple pleasures? Perhaps this is hyperbolic, but it really seemed like every meal, every activity and every conversation we had together was a simple pleasure. What sweetened the weekend? Warm beds, autumn trees and an absence of anxiety meant that there was space to purely *enjoy*, uninhibited from the noise and (yes, this was a privilege) from the to-do list. We went on runs, visited lookouts, enjoyed almond croissants and coffee for breakfast, we made pesto pasta, I fell asleep during our long-awaited viewing of *Harry Potter and the Goblet of Fire* (sorry, Clare, I'm unashamedly diurnal), we drank cheap Aldi wine (it's a blessing to not have a refined palate), we danced, visited op-shops and talked *a lot*. The few weeks prior to leaving, we'd assembled a list of talking points. While this may appear inorganic, the plan was effective, and we traded wisdom, advice, admonishment and encouragement.

Simply put, this was the first weekend in a long while that I felt light-hearted. A final simple pleasure? Full, nourishing friendships. Clare is a kindred friend, one who so easily sees the best in me, and I in her.

* * *

Something I'd been struggling with was a loss of a sense of selfhood and identity. My psychologist authenticated the fact that I'd lived the past two years extremely dependent on another person, our identities had become entwined. Without him and the daily habits we'd built up together, I needed to begin again. So yeah, I've needed to assert my individuality through habits and rituals that were my own. I've been grieving a lost partner and hoped-for future and needed help to fall in love with life again.

Truthfully, I am insecure about relationships. Intellectually, I know that I am loved. Emotionally, I've needed assurance of this, and simple pleasures and the mysterious passage of time have been a balm to the prickliness of circumstance. Without the comforts and familiarity I'd relied on for a long time, new practices had to be cultivated. My hope is that I fall in love with life again by falling in love with God again, by seeing His hand in the wonders of life – His creativity in creation, in flavours, scents, colours, people, stories. Navigating life is a highly internal affair and as I sit, stand and walk, I hope that simple pleasures will nourish me and lead me to nourish and care for others. My God is a compassionate God, and He invites us to be still and know Him. I'm learning that I know Him best when I partake in simple pleasures that lead me to rest, love authentically and savour life as a child of God.

June 2022

I'd like to close with a wish – something I hope to generate and cultivate, a posture I hope will be encouraged by the people who orbit my life. Through patience, gratitude, solemnity and delight, my wish is that the fog will be blown out of my soul.

Humanity knows all too well that paths are not always pleasant or peaceful; light and joy are often eclipsed by circumstance; bitterness and grief may cloud one's view. But is it not the contrast between light and dark that makes the light all the more bright? I'm not certain the season has turned yet, but I hope to be surprised when I notice the unclouded sky. Noticing simple pleasures experienced by others and constructed by myself has ushered in strength and calm. There is loveliness to be glad about in this world, as remembered by Anne Shirley, and gladness fortifies the soul.

7 July 2022

My simple pleasure today has been observing the incremental changes in colour in the trees outside. Contemplating the shared disbursement of green, orange and yellow leaves is making me shed tears, I think because it feels a little like me right now. Change has been ever so slow, with some days feeling like milestones, others like painful regression, and today isn't particularly wonderful. A high anxiety day, without pockets of slowness or joy, but in the perpetual grind of these days that bubble over with activity and emotion, I've found pleasure in stopping just for a moment, at 3.16 pm, and witnessing the leaves shake in the wind.

I'm tired. I've been tired for a while. The slightest thing will tip me off the edge into worry and fear, relationships feel strained, work and study demand so much, but as my good friend Clare will often remind me, I'm with me for life, and if my cup feels empty and in need of love and affection, I can begin by adding in a few drops myself. Drops of lightness, of comfort, of silliness, indulgence, productivity, quiet, noise, a good cup of tea can do the trick (if drunk slowly . . . I'm learning how to slowly enjoy tea and coffee, a difficult task when one has extremely resilient heat sensors in their mouth).

Serendipitously, Jess Gillam's song "Dappled Light" played while I was staring at the trees, and goodness me that *really* tipped me over the edge into tears of thankfulness. Sometimes the antidote to intense anxiety, worry, fear and sadness is stopping. It's no secret, I know, but I had to remind myself. Writing this has reminded me. Clearly I need continual reminding after four months of sporadic writing. Writing this has been a simple pleasure. How appropriate.

* * *

The conclusion. To be honest with your own soul and sense of self is both onerous and exhausting. But when you are with you for life, the task is necessary. Bitterness and painful memories continue to bubble up in my heart, and the fear of loneliness and unworthiness are shadows in my mind. Nobody is obligated to cheer me up or be the balm to my tender heart, so where can I find a sense of peace?

The world is very big, and we are very small. When we stand in awe and wonder before both soft and powerful visitations of natural wonders, sweetness seeps into the soul. So we wade through great waters, praying for the tempest to settle and unsettle us, and as we come across life's simple pleasures, peace will surely come.

References

Baird, Julia. 2020. *Phosphorescence: On Awe, Wonder and Things That Sustain You When the World Goes Dark*. Sydney: 4th Estate.

Mongomery, L.M. 1907. *Anne of Green Gables*. Boston: L.C. Page & Co.

Oldfield, Elizabeth. 2017. *The Sacred*. Recorded in London, UK. Podcast. https://podcasts.apple.com/gb/podcast/the-sacred/id1326888108.

Milnes, Tim, and Nicolas Tredell. 2009. *William Wordsworth: The Prelude*. Basingstoke: Palgrave Macmillan.

Nocturnal Sounds

Vanessa Vu

Do you hear them, caught between the waking and the hour?
The peach-lipped sun caresses your downy head
but you turn away from the birdsong, frog song, shower song,
for the promise of one more minute.
Minute by minute you replay the sounds; nocturnal, safe, soft
    as cotton.
Smells like cotton? Cotton and dreams – your favourite smell.
But back to the sounds.
Pens and pencils scribbling away – the baton is passed and now
    you can rest.
Cars swishing past the living room window,
absent thoughts skimming the rain-slicked road,
their headlights muted by the curtain. Your face safely
    concealed,
comfortably sitting between world and home
with the rain playing tunes on the windowpane.
Dad's car radio pours into the night,
running along telephone poles smooth as silk
and you drift with the tyres rolling you
away from piano lessons towards bedtime.
Pages rustling as they did when words were made indelible.

The clink of a teacup finding its place in the saucer.
Faded whispers upon the walls; content, after-party ones
when no one needs to do the dishes after.
This place was louder when you were young
and your head was filled with carnival rides
and merry-go-rounds dancing round. The lights were brighter,
     too.
Now when you sit on the train, flashing in and out of tunnels,
you momentarily hear the echo of the fairground
when the tunnel swallows the light
and you are given brief respite.

But now the light is back
and the birdsong, frog song, shower song plays once more.
You get your things and head out the door, aching for that
     "just one more",
though you need not worry.
You need only look around the corner to find it
just where you left it.

The Sky Is a Teenage Girl

Zoe Morris

hey, did you see
when the teenage girl
who is the god of the sky
flung gold glitter onto the horizon
like a party dress?

did you see when she blew
globular bubbles of purple and pink
onto a grey background?

she tops her art class, she
has an eye for composition, she
just needs more
restraint.

sometimes when she's bored she draws doodles
onto the margins of the sky
and the clouds swirl to meet her pen.

did you see her love heart?
her elephant?

her rose?
as all children know, cloud-gazing is a witness of the divine.

sometimes when she's mad, bolts of plasma will fall out of her
like porcupine darts
and her skin will grow grey as despair.

the sunset is for desire.

above all, watch carefully when she falls asleep
and the stars emerge from the black depths –
for these are her dreams,
and they glow brighter and more precious
than diamonds.

Wind Chimes/Pearl Earrings

A.E. Leighton

In my (now former) bedroom, I hear the distant ring of wind chimes float on the gentle breeze. A window set unpleasingly into the opposite blue wall breaks the confining atmosphere of the room. The wooden sill is dusty and disregarded; it may be my fault. I perch on the edge of my bed and gaze into the equally unclean stand mirror on the windowsill. Here is the makeshift vanity where I brush my unkempt hair and put on a pair of pearl earrings. Still, it is the only opening for me to see the outside world. I slide the pane open. It creaks, protests that it is being maimed. It must have been opened hundreds of times, many a time by a different girl trapped in her room.

I am sitting down, perhaps reading a book or felling seams with a tiny needle. My door hangs half-open. Outside is an unfathomably short distance out of reach. But when the chimes ring, I touch the unattainable wonders that lie beyond the window. The chimes remind me that I am not bound to be isolated in this powder blue room forever. I put down my book, or needlework, and peer into the cloudless sky. My view has always been obstructed by some unsightly artificial thing – a flyscreen, verandah or the battered corrugated fence of my neighbour.

The chimes tinkle again. I return to what I was doing beforehand. All the while, I sit and surmise where the chimes come from. They must be a short distance away. Yet, they appear as phantom melodies from a faraway place. I could go down the street, catch a bus . . . but I cannot. Such simple escapades are unfeasible. Because I need to ask, but asking requires me to speak my thoughts in this intolerant house. Thus, I remain in my room, forbidden to venture out.

I am aware of my presence in my bedroom, and simultaneously my mind wanders to a fantasy land. Or, more tangibly, I sit in my room with no company, but a few streets over, someone I know is indulging in blissful leisure. We can hold no knowledge of any life external to our own, but imaginative distance gives an almost perfect sense of another person's life.

For here I am in my blue room, so removed from the decadence of teenage folly. I am a maiden locked in a tower; the shabby window offers me a glimpse of the expansive world without – if only I could reach out, out, out, to the vivid greenery . . . I know that while I lay sleepless others indulge in late-night parties, staggering in drunken stupors among the twinkle of garden lights. But it is more than treading to the door and running into the damp, open air. I cannot catch the bus; I cannot go to the party. So I resort to imagination. So I listen to the subtle cascade of wind chimes and conjure an ideal life.

When the wind chimes cease, I do not notice. I carry on with whatever I am occupied with. The next day, it all repeats. I live in a constant cycle of temporary pursuit and an ever-present desire to escape. But the wind chimes bring a faint melody, a small pleasure breaking the monotony of my confined existence. Even now, in the roar of the metropolis, I remember the delicate wind chimes carried through the air – like a bubble, it surfaces momentarily and then disappears.

All this is a memory to me now, and I can only write in such indeterminate terms. It is a blessing to forget the feeling of deep-rooted confinement, but a curse to lose the sensation of an integral part of my past.

* * *

Losing one half of my pearl earrings is comparatively worse than losing both earrings. Like shoes, if both are lost, then you may dispense of the set. But losing one half is the bane of my existence. Now I have one pearl earring with none to match. They shall sit in my drawer, desolate, reduced to a mere lonesome white bead. They despair that they can no longer decorate my ears.

I think I lost the earring while trying on clothes. I have always been clumsy. It was not until afterwards, when I got home, that I realised one ear was undecorated. I suppose there is an omnipresent force of give and take; I decided to buy the red floral dress that I had tried on. But the lost pearl earring still tugs at the edges of my brain.

Why should I lament? It is no great loss. Those earrings were probably not genuine pearl anyway. I bought them an indeterminate period ago at the Royal Adelaide Show. In the grand scheme of things, I will likely forget that I ever lost the one earring at all. However, this afternoon, I shall cry and be bitter as much as I please. I liked those earrings very much;

even if they were imitating those real white growths plucked from the moist insides of an oyster. Imagine – wearing pearls is like wearing a memento crafted by the sea. Someone long ago picked up a dull shell, thinking it was a rock, and cracked it open to reveal a priceless milky drop. Now we wear pearls around our neck, ears, fingers, carrying nature's riches on our bodies.

It's not that I do not have pearls. I have not one, but two pearl necklaces. Understandably, I do not wear them often. They are far too precious. Ever and anon I will take a peek at those strands – shimmering, glowing white beads of the oyster. Then I will put them back and forget I have them in the first place. Simultaneously, I wish I could wear those pearl necklaces more often. They are simply too good to be eternally stored away. They are meant to be worn and appreciated. I am like a child – too greedy, wanting everything to myself but also wanting to show off my precious trinkets.

But I lose earrings and break necklaces. The pendant choker I broke long ago lies languidly in my wardrobe. In art history, the girl next to me broke her silver necklace and it fell to the floor. I suppose I am lucky that the choker was second-hand. Still I mourn that unworn necklace, never to fulfil its one purpose. Pearl necklaces and pendant chokers; a cycle of buying, breaking, trying to find a faithful imitation.

When I visit the antique store, I am always struck by the variety of jewellery. They scintillate and dance under the bright gallery lights. I lean against the glass case and observe those priceless stones. Inlaid in gold or silver, around a velvet band, mounted on a wedding ring, hanging about a latticed hoop. I wish to pluck them from the case and try them on myself.

And then I would imagine who wore them, and why they are now enclosed and waiting to be sold. Those jewels were once someone's heirloom. Now they shall be passed into a stranger's hand.

I buy my jewellery cheap, at the op shops. They cost five dollars or so and satisfy my craving for shiny trinkets. There are dainty earrings, long necklaces, ornate brooches, oversized rings; whatever seems pleasing to my senseless tastes. I wear them proudly. Perhaps they were cherished by their previous owners, but soon grew to be redundant. So then I snatch them up. My instincts are sometimes described as being crow-like. That is rather accurate, for I swoop at anything that is bright and glimmering.

In fact, I sometimes prefer op shop jewellery to the polished marvels in antique store cases. The op shops have *things*; things that we can touch, wear, display. They are charming paradoxes, misshapen and exquisitely crafted, the priceless artefacts made of Bakelite. I do not care that what I find in op shops are considered cheap and amateurish. All that matters is that they give me an inexplicable pleasure.

What is life if not plucking out shiny things? I cannot imagine living only by practical measures. Those pearl earrings satiated my aesthetics, and now that one is lost, my senses are imbalanced. Thus I lament. We are made to hold onto little trifles. We are supposed to be surrounded by colour and shine. I could not stand my bare walls, so I cut up pictures from magazines and taped them up. Now when I cannot sleep, I stare at the scattering of small paintings above. And I am grateful that now I can decorate my walls. I no longer have to face a powder blue abyss.

When I sift through displays of jewellery, metal strikes metal and they ring – like my wind chimes of yore. Another accidental melody.

The next time I go to the op shops, I will find another pair of pearl earrings.

Brewed

Zara

What's brewing in my heart is love
for you.
Let me pour it out,   there will be enough for two.
Come sit,
and you'll see
these steeping leaves   were chipped off you and me.
Come sit,
and I'll sweeten   the dregs   of my heart-brewed tea.

Come sip,
and   feel the honey-heat   coursing through you.
It'll scorch you clean, my love, for you.

Come sip,
spout-to-spout   I'll fill   you up.

Come tomorrow,
and I'll sit   and sip
the tea you've brewed for me.
Till then –
my heart sits empty.

The Little Beach

Sarah Nicole Ambrose

The sound of the waves gently brushing against the shore is almost irresistible as I creep along the path from the house, a KeepCup full of fresh, hot coffee in my hand. It's early, the sky still dark. Ahead of me, I can just barely make out the shape of the others as they step carefully through the grass and down the stairs. I follow behind, just as carefully.

And then we are there. On the little beach. Just us. Settling on the cold sand. Waiting for the sun.

In this moment, with the sand and the sea and the sun just beginning to peek out over the horizon, it's easy to forget that anything else exists. I am entirely in the here and now. Maybe for the first time in my life. I watch the rainbow of colours as the sky turns from black to a combination of blue and pink and gold, broken up by the fluffy white clouds that have now become visible.

We picked a good sunrise – perhaps the best one – to wake up early for, and I feel so much pity for the others who stayed in bed. I'm running on maybe two hours of sleep at this point, but the beauty, the peace and the coffee have given me an energy like nothing else ever could. I wouldn't have missed this for anything.

All good things must end, and all too soon the sun is most of the way up and the sky is bright. And the rest of the group drift back over to the house, ready to get a few extra hours in before breakfast.

There are just two of us left on the beach. We've experienced something so magical that sleep is now impossible for us. So we do the only thing that makes sense on an empty beach: we sink into the calm waves, surprisingly warm for just after sunrise in early March.

We float.

And it feels like heaven.

December

Hannah Roux

Give me a long, white-hot December,
twisted and dipped in shining pools.
I'll take for wreaths the taste of water
and for stars the flannel flowers.

Give me white butterflies storming
for snowdrift in its blaze,
the laugh of seashells thrashing
foam-crested on green waves.

I'll even take the heat of noon –
vertical, crisp, the flatness of light –
if on the blue sky also bloom
two crimson wings, a bird in flight.

Summer Water

Juan Pablo Guevara Morales

The clock strikes five
computers go off
striding, running
rushing for that first summer swim

Heading to the edge of the land
meeting the sea,
the fruitful splash of white water
rinses it all away

A week is dead and gone
eyes closed
weightless limbs
in an open sea
forever floating
forever free

The Lady of the Lake

Tom Williamson

The horses' hooves echoed in the green tunnel of foliage. The troop wandered through the Queen's Forest behind Erin as nightfall crept over them. She rode on a well-groomed destrier that towered several hands higher than the other stallions. Her well-kept hair swayed across her golden royal epaulettes with the motion of the horse. A gentle whistling noise filled the space in the air between the clip-clopping of hooves. Erin drew the air deep into her lungs through pursed lips.

Dozens of fireflies eased out of the neighbouring forestry and swarmed the path. They danced around the horses, providing enough light to see by and warming the hearts and hopes of the weary travellers.

Erin turned to watch her lights roll out in echelons through the group. They flew around the heads of Bran, Glyn, Mari, Olwen, Dai, Ceri, Cadi, Maddox, and to the two young boys at the rear.

The young ones stared in amazement at the insects that glimmered like stars.

"I heard they got thorns!" Dyl whispered. He tightened his grip around the reins.

"I don't care about thorns," Wyn replied, "It's the tramplin' I'm concerned about."

"Why does she want us to go to the Cewri anyway? Seems like a rather daft thing to do. Don't you think?"

"I suppose that's why we're getting paid. Stealing fruit from giants."

"I'd hardly call it pay. I'm going to leave my sick Ma all alone only to come back no bigger than a foot tall, smelling like giant's feet, just for a few lousy coins."

"We're not going to steal anything," said a weary sounding voice in front of them.

The two youngest troopers looked at each other. Maddox had hardly uttered a word the entire trip from Caernarfon.

"Then what are we going to do, Mister . . . ahh . . . Maddox . . . Sir?" asked Wyn.

"Negotiate." His voice crackled and sounded thin.

"What do we have to offer?" asked Dyl. There was discernment in his voice and for the first time, Maddox turned to look at them.

"Two young boys," Maddox replied with a smirk.

Wyn's grip got even tighter, the pressure causing the reigns to tense and his horse to rear and whinny. Mari, who rode next to Maddox, rolled her eyes and gave him a light tap on the shoulder. Her brunette hair was laced with a unique streak of orange. It looked like strawflowers in a field after heavy rain. Maddox and Mari turned to check if Wyn had stabilised his mare.

"Watch yourself, lad, she's a timid one," Maddox said, "Slow movements and never pull tight. Beca there is an old-timer, she knows what she wants. Haste is the Diafol's currency."

Dyl's brows furrowed at the mention of such a strange name. Before he could open his mouth to ask, Lili slowed her pace and interrupted.

"Don't worry about his ancient talk. He says a lot of things in the old tongue. Especially with a tongue as old as his."

Wyn relaxed his grip and returned to a gentle trot. The Cewri had terrorised his dreams for as long as he could remember. The thought of encountering them in the flesh struck a terror through him, a fear that burrowed down to his bones. The image of those monstrous beings flashed in dark paint across the canvas of his mind.

"We trade our services for their life fruit," said Maddox. "Those giants might hoard the fauna that produces such a flower, but they're not the smartest bunch. They need all the help they can get."

He looked at the rest of the crew in front of him as he spoke.

"Erin up there, she will ward off the locusts for two harvests. Bran will draw moisture into the earth. Glyn and Mari will burn off the dry grass to protect their home from wildfire. Olwen changes the constellations. Then when the time comes, the giants will know the perfect time for harvest. For our help, they'll let us take some of the fruit."

"And Lili and Cadi?" asked Dyl.

"They will sing to them while we work, plucking at the air around them to create powerful symphonies that calm the giants."

"It seems to work when you're after a handsome payment and trying to make it out alive," added Lili.

"What will you do?" asked Wyn.

Maddox took a deep breath and closed his eyes for a moment, then vines descended from above. They curled above the horses' heads and Dyl, Wyn and Maddox came to a stop. The vines twisted themselves around the gentleman's elderly frame wrapping around his torso, stiffening into a back support that swayed with the trot of the horse. The gentleman could sit up straight again, the weight of his shoulders now less of a problem.

"I will grow their seedlings up out of the ground," Maddox said.

Astonishment washed over Wyn and Dyl for the second time that day.

"And why are we here?" asked Dyl.

The boys squeezed their legs together urging their horses on again. Wyn's mare, however, surged forward, sending him backward almost flat on his back.

"You are young and dextrous. You're here to help unpack the mules and answer to any quest she might have." Maddox nodded towards Erin at the front. Her fireflies still floated around the troop.

"Plus, you never know. Perhaps you might learn something." He glanced towards Wyn who was shifting uncomfortably on his unpredictable horse. "Provided you make it."

As night settled in, Erin drew in more fireflies and before long it was time to stop for the night. They settled on the soft ground where the forest met the Peryglus Sea. Wyn and Dyl set up tents and carted around cooking utensils. They scurried like worker bees making a new home for their queen.

Mari knelt next to some gathered kindling. She clicked her fingers and blew gently through the air where the noise had occurred. Tiny embers emerged from nothingness, leaping down from her mouth into the pit. The campfire was roaring with heat in a matter of seconds. She rose and looked down at what she had created.

The inexperienced ones observed her from across the camp. Dyl could see the embers flickering in front of her glassy eyes; eyes still filled with amazement. Who knew how many times she had done that? She was so good at it. And yet, in her eyes there was something else as she pondered the flames: fear. Like the fire still held something over her.

"That's the humblest dragon if I've ever seen one," Wyn said. Dyl felt the punch on his arm and heard his friend chuckle.

The boys finished setting the final tent before joining Maddox and the rest of the troop for supper. They crunched on bread and dried meats, while a pot of water came to boil on the fire.

Maddox reached into his breast pocket and pulled out a handful of seeds. He parted some space in the soil between his feet and lay the seeds there, then replaced the dirt and closed his eyes. Green stalks emerged from the ground and waved in the firelight. Small lavender petals completed them. Hopes that belonged to earth, brought to fruition by the hand of a traveller. Maddox plucked the petals and crushed them between his ragged hands.

There was a sleepy silence about the group as they sipped comforting lavender tea.

"What's so good about life fruit anyways?" Wyn asked, breaking the tranquillity.

Glyn and Olwen both looked towards Erin to answer the question.

"The nobility in Caernarfon are very fond of it," Erin replied.

"Is it sweet or something?"

"It is rather sweet. But that is not its most attractive feature. It has certain . . . properties, that they're fond of."

"Such as?"

"Each fruit can add a decade to your life."

The troop didn't seem fazed by such an idea, but Wyn and Dyl sat with their mouths agape.

"A whole decade! Why are they trusting us to go and get them?" asked Dyl.

"Because they know we don't want to eat them."

There were gentle laughs and smiles around the fire. And with that conclusion, the laughter turned to yawns and the rest of the party, including Erin, stood up and sought their needed rest. Wyn, Dyl and Maddox remained.

"Each of them has their reasons for not wanting the fruit," Maddox whispered across the crackling flames.

"What about you?" asked Wyn.

The old trooper leaned in closer. The flickering light wavered across his face. The exhaustion of his years showed in the grey specs of his eyes.

"I have lived a long enough life to know I don't need any more decades, but I have heard a story that makes decades feel like precious seconds that shouldn't be wasted." He let out a deep sigh and lowered his voice.

"Have you heard of the promise of Llyn y Fan Fach and the Creu?"

The two of them nodded intently.

"Listen carefully and I'll tell you a tale . . ."

* * *

The wind was too strong. It lashed against his dry lips and pestered his freezing fingers. The traveller was the only one in its path. There were no trees to sway up there, no monk chimes to receive its song. He was the wind's only instrument, and anger was its song. It beat down on him until he could no longer walk up those chiselled cliffs. Whipping gusts lacerated his ears and punished his entire existence.

A primal scream filled the air as the power of the storm brought him to his knees. Involuntary tears rolled down his wind-chafed cheeks and he dragged himself the rest of the way to the mountain pass. He gritted his teeth and scrunched his eyes closed. Dried blood covered the traveller's makeshift bandages and underneath them, open wounds went down to the bone. His wrappings touched raw exposed nerves and gritty pebbles infiltrated his sores. His forearms were a burned forest from the dragon's breath. Yet the promise of reward outweighed every dose of pain.

The winds would not stop for a courageous man. The howling reminded him of other more courageous men in battle, screaming at the pain of dismembered legs and charred faces.

The determined traveller inched his way to the top of the mountain and there he sought refuge before he tumbled over the crest and slid down its steep descent.

The other side of the mountain was peaceful. Strangely . . . oddly . . . eerily peaceful. Green carpeted the cirque, and at its centre lay the dark lake: the eye of the mountain. Lying perfectly still, unblinking. The wind not only quietened but seemed to stop altogether.

His cheeks flushed with warmth in the calm air. He ran his shattered hands through the lush grass and the fresh drops of dew stung in his palms.

He regained his stance like a young fowl walking for the first time. Aches conquered the wretched body, and each step brought a searing flame to his knees. With cautious steps, he began his descent towards the water.

A soft hum echoed round the valley and brought calm to his wind-struck skin.

Darkness pervaded that water. The surface consumed the sunlight and drowned it far beneath the bedrock.

The hum became more present. It took on a sweet melody and high-pitched notes wandered over his eardrums. It sounded like taught horsehair gliding over a perfectly tuned viola. The sound became increasingly more beautiful and he was drawn to it like a moth to a candle. A moth who does not care if they are burned because the light is so magnificent.

Local animals shifted towards the noise. Tabby foxes emerged from burrows and, entranced, walked towards the lake. They drank out of it and were warmed by it. The dusting of snow on their fur began to melt.

The descent was far gentler.

Shallow creeks ran smoothly through the mossy valley, so clear you could see the riverbed beneath them. He cupped his hands to drink. It too was warm; it tasted pure and like honey. He knew immediately that he wanted more.

The hum became louder and clearer. A choir singing at their highest tone.

As he came to the lake's edge, he noticed bees and butterflies encompassed the shore. Steam evaporated off the charcoal water, volcanic heat radiated from the surface and the traveller was convinced he had found the gates to heaven or perhaps the entrance to hell.

The serenity burst.

The music stopped.

The lake began to ripple and then waves undulated across its tense surface. A huge spire of divine water erupted out of the centre. The music returned and the humming became deafening. He collapsed at its vibration and looked up in awe.

A figure rose from the dark jet-stream in cobalt blue. Droplets streamed off her quasi-formed body in supple spheres. Her skin turned to porcelain and her features melted into place. With a roll of her neck, she fluttered open her eyes to reveal the amethyst gems that rested there.

Giant platforms of water developed in front of her, grander than the steps of a palace. As she descended, organic material emerged and combined to clothe her. She was laced in green leaves and the seams of her garments were lined with daffodils. The most beautiful lady in the world walked down the aquatic steps and offered him her hand.

The simple motion of her reaching out her arm was like watching the most intense sunset in the world. He took her hand and kissed it gently with lips that were near sewn together, as she placed her other on his cheek. Her voice was hypnotic when she spoke. She offered him what he sought. Everlasting life and everlasting pleasure. All his desires and all of his needs. She offered him the promise of each other's care for the rest of time. He gave his acceptance graciously.

She led him into the warm lake from which she had emerged. The aquatic steps had turned to volcanic rock. He drew in a breath as his neck reached level with the water. She smiled and told him to let go. The following steps were effortless and the transition from air to water was unnoticeable. The water was as pleasant as the Isles of Bach. Beneath the surface she took his hand and showed him the way to her palace.

* * *

"Where is she now?" asked Dyl.

"She's gone."

Silence returned.

"What happened to your promise?"

"That's gone too." He cleared his throat before continuing.

The sound of insects pervaded the air and his thoughts seemed to intertwine with one another.

"We stayed together for eight hundred years. For a mortal, some would say that is everlasting."

The two boys watched on as he held his eyes closed and rubbed at his temples. The age of his voice was now truly apparent.

As Maddox spoke, he clenched his right fist and held his eyes shut. The two boys wanted to ask more, but they questioned with their attention alone.

"After all those years, all those centuries, I loved her with everything that I had. But my mind began to decay in a body that stayed young. She loved me back, but I saw pity in her eyes. Not just for a few years but for centuries. Time had corrupted my soul." A blanket of tears began to gloss over his eyes. "So, I chose to leave."

Dyl was confused. He had never heard of anyone coming out of the Creu realm alive.

"How did you break a promise with a creature of that power?" Dyl asked.

"I don't know," the old man responded. He opened his palms to reveal severe discolouring on his palms. "But it was not without severe pain. She seemed to try to love me more. Not because she wanted me to stay, but because she needed to punish me. It was my weakness. She knew that love would be my one true master. A subservient mortal in the path of a powerful goddess. Love drove my inner monologue and extinguished the last spark of my sanity."

The fire spat, the coals growing weaker as cold air returned to the pit.

"Evidently, she chose not to kill me."

"Do you miss her?" asked Wyn.

"Every day. I think that is the most severe part of my punishment. I remember each and every day I spent with her. My mind is filled to the brim with the details of our lives. From the number of lashes on her eyes to the texture of her skin, they are burned into my memory." He opened his palm to reveal a daffodil growing to maturity. "But in the end even the most beautiful flower eventually wilts."

The two boys sat attentively, listening to all the words he could possibly offer. Amazed by the powers in his hands. How could such an extraordinary group of people all manage to find each other? They all seemed to have something so significant to offer, and yet here they were travelling to the land of giants, to do trade with them on behalf of the Caernarfon elite. Such raw and beautiful powers. All unique and seemingly special to each that held them.

Maddox kept his arm outstretched, as the daffodil's yellow leaves browned and decayed.

He reclosed his palm, rose from his seat and spoke his final words before bidding them goodnight.

"Mortals seek many desires," he said, staring at where the parched leaves lay on the ground, "but there is only one that rises above them all. The desire to live. To live . . . forever."

Exhausted from the day of travelling and remembering, he turned away from the young troopers and murmured just loud enough for them both to hear: "Some desires ought to be left solely as desires."

Maddox walked towards his tent, and as he left, a small green stalk shot up from beneath the dehydrated leaves and another daffodil began to grow.

Silence surrounded the campfire for several minutes and eventually the boys followed suit, taking themselves to bed.

They shared a tent with the entrance drawn open, letting some of the heat from the fire into their tiny space. Dyl sat looking out as Wyn nestled into his sleep. With the thought of decades upon decades of life resting in his mind, he looked out upon the moon above the Peryglus. He thought of his bed-ridden mother. The insignificance of the coins he pursued to keep her alive a few more months.

He thought about the Creu and the stories that surrounded her, their ambiguity and the fear that they struck up in him. He thought of the beauty he had seen today, the gifts that these people had. The fondness he found in those simple gifts and pleasures. The thought of living forever sent a shiver down his spine. And in that moment the shiver spoke a truth to him, that which he did not fully understand. But he instinctively held out his hands, like a monk before ritual or a beggar in the lowly streets of Caernarfon.

With two palms open and his thoughts at ease, he drew his hands in and placed them on his chest.

The moon came closer and the tide rose.

He released his hands and the water settled.

The sky lit up with the amber glow of fatherly guidance and the stars blanketed the earth like a maternal embrace.

The Lady of the Lake Map, Tom Williamson

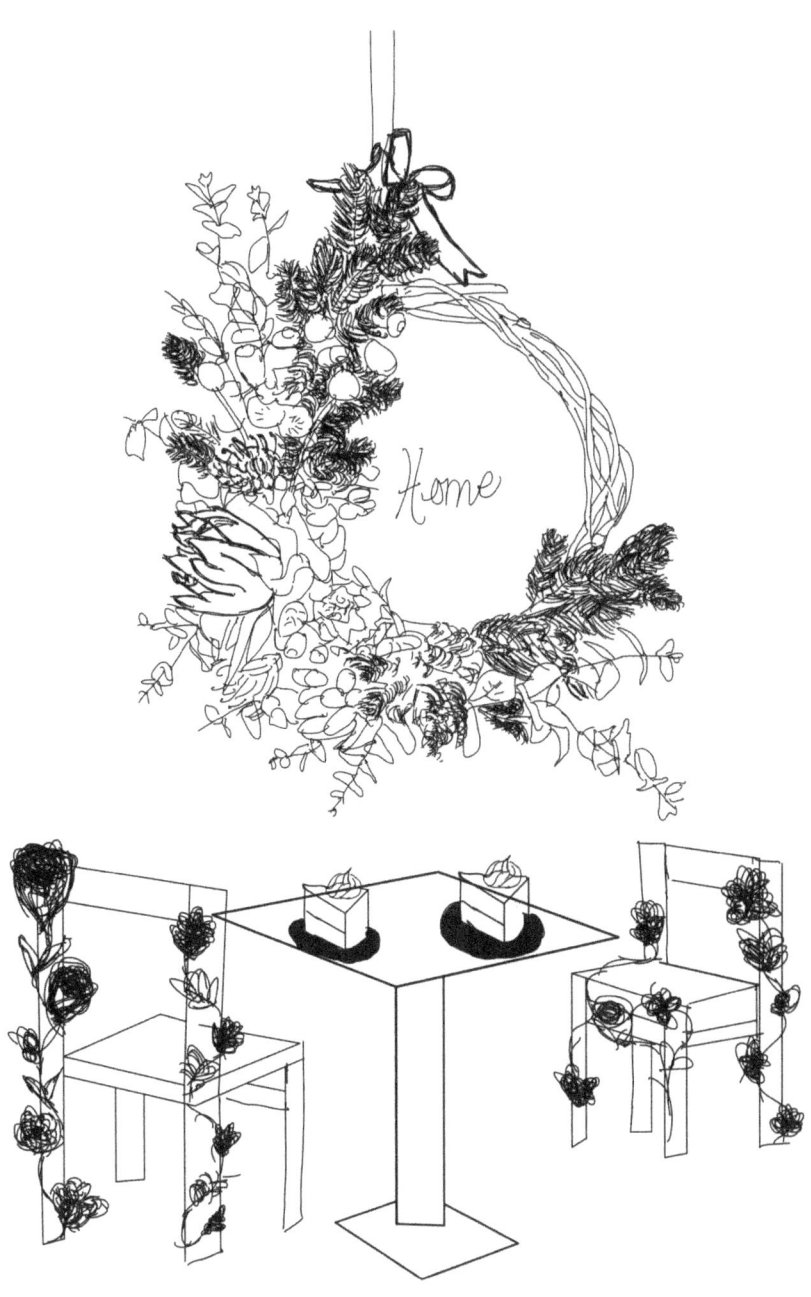

Home Sweet Home, Memi Adams

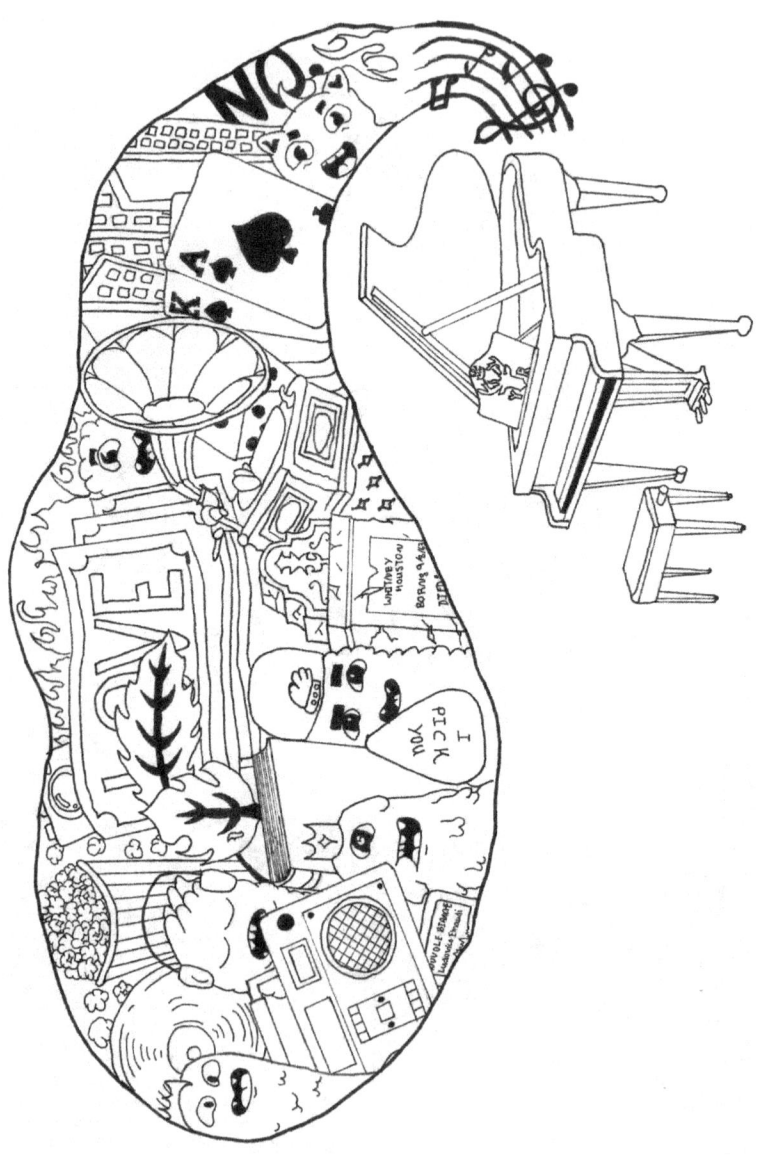

Für Elise, Yusur Razaqe

Bird & Telephone Pole, Nicholas J.J. Smith

Grocery Shop 1, Lindsay Rui, Charles Liang and Cecile Zhang

Grocery Shop 2, Lindsay Rui, Charles Liang and Cecile Zhang

Home, Yasodara Puhule-Gamayalage

Hiding in Plain Sight

James Puterflam

The simpler the pleasure, the easier it's attained.
Without great effort or time spent in vain.
Present at the instant without planning or pain.
Overlooked, undesired, too simple, too plain.

Inextinguishable and everlasting,
The magic pudding of good passings,
Possession doesn't exist, it's all just momentary,
What could be attractive about pleasure rudimentary?

It's available with your breath or very next step,
Or colours blazing bright by dazzling sunlight,
As is a tango with water, tempt for the occasion,
Soaked upon lips or gliding down hips,

Morning birds rapture the church of life's existence,
Thoughts without limits roll like waves out from the sea,
Open, free, spontaneous like clouds upon a breeze,
A space-like mind at ease with whatever it sees,

If simple pleasures are simple, then why may one not find them?
For they're given no importance, as such "things" are not desirable.
Seeing them not, they're left out to rot.
A corpse, memories, untouched they are forgot.

Things We Loved and Lost

Sharmila Jayasinghe

One. Two. Three. I count, stopping at twenty-three.

I think I am accurate, maybe I missed one or two or added one or two but that is the sum of it, a rough number of words he spoke today.

Yesterday it was less. Exactly ten. Six in the morning and four at night.

Twenty-three: I take today to be a good day but there's no time for more.

He is silent again. Just tunes of snores that are not words.

The lack of words, the lack of his words makes me feel different. Empty.

When a word is said it is not dead, it begins to live. Dickinson is right.
His words said, they begin to live.
His words said, I begin to live.

"Mehndi," I remember the very first word he spoke, directed at me. We were in a group. Everyone listening to everyone, everyone talking to everyone. He was two people away from me. He leant on the bar counter and looked at my hands. "Mehndi," he said, sliding past the two in between us. He held my hand, gently tracing the fading pattern with his finger. He was older. His eyes gentle. I didn't feel unsafe. "This is an ancient art. *Mendhika* is a Sanskrit word. It's a Vedic custom. Henna, the colour that made these patterns on your hands, is taken from a plant: *Lawsonia inermis*. The leaves are dried and crushed to make a powder. It was also used as a hair dye. Still is. A fabric dye as well." There was something sweet and reassuring about the way he spoke even if he didn't speak sweet things to reassure. I easily became his voice-hearer.

One time I snuck into a lecture of his. He used big words. They jumped out of his mouth and vibrated around the hall. *Occidentalism. Orientalism. Hybridity. Postcolonialism.* I wrote them down on the back of a Woolworths docket and brought it back home with me. His Sinhala words were rounded and sharp; his English was always square. Sometimes I barely understood what he said, but I listened. I liked the sound of his voice, deep and clear. Beautiful. I thought if Elvis Presley spoke instead of singing, he would sound just like that. I watched his Adam's apple, large and protruding, dance to the rhythm of his words. Later when we kissed, like a careful painter I gently brushed my finger over it. Felt it move inside his neck, a hidden treasure of some kind. Sometimes we sipped *saruwath*, sitting in a small eatery in Seven Hills watching the day unfold. The afternoon train stopped on the other side of the road. People emptied out and climbed the stairs, which took them to the bus stop right in front of us. The empty train slowly slithered out of sight. "More than eighty people died in the Granville train accident. It was the fault of the rail tracks. It was the train running from the Blue Mountains. Full of office and school crowds. January 18th," he said on January 18th. "Exactly fifteen years ago today." Something always triggered within him, like flicking on a light switch. He always had something to say about things we saw in Toongabbie, of trains, tracks, wheels, people and their histories. He talked. I listened, wetting my throat with the overly sweet syrupy drink. Every time I wandered over to the only window in our living room, he looked over his glasses and smiled. He had pushed his writing table against the window, "So *you* could see outside," he said. Out the window I could see roofs, an endless lot of roofs. Big and small, tiled and not. Flat and boxy, and ones that weren't roofs at all. "The old temple at Corinth is the oldest building that has terracotta tiles, historical evidence." When I was at the window, he carefully followed my eyes, waiting to see where they halted. Then he explained what I saw. "Red-necked stints migrate south to escape the winter in Siberia. They fly back and forth over fifty thousand kilometres because they breed on the Arctic tundra," he said one time. I didn't see a bird out the window, but he thought I did. He talked and talked. I sat on his lap and looked out trying to find the bird he thought I saw. It didn't matter that I couldn't find the bird. The picture his words painted was enough for me to see. "Arctic tundra" left an earworm; I felt happy the tiny red-necked stints could escape the harsh winter and find warmth near my home. I thought of the birds till late that night. Till he came to bed, and we made love. His words always sank in and took me somewhere else, migrated with birds, painted intricate patterns on hands, or grieved for an unknown dead. I never counted his words then. There wouldn't have been enough numbers or time.

I can't quite remember how his words transformed into meaningless sounds or turned to be like a tangled mass of yarn inside my head, a lump of loops with no end and no beginning. He spoke at all the wrong times; when I was bouncing on an exercise ball in the birthing room, when I was attempting to salvage Charmaine Solomon's burnt tandoori tikka chicken, when the breast pump was on, or the vacuum cleaner, the hair drier, or the electric toothbrush, when I was watching *Friends* or *Home and Away*, or when my limbs were too tired not to curl up and sleep.

Long after we had stopped watching trains and people, and drinking sweet syrupy *saruwath* in Toongabbie, I remember one time watching his mouth work. He was chewing and talking.

Crunch went cornflakes inside his mouth.
Milk snowed out with his words, landing in a pattern on the
    wooden table.
A microfiber cloth with vinegar?
Earth Choice? Not too harsh.
Mr Sheen? Would that be better?
Need to clean before it sticks.

Finish feeding Mia.

Find cloth.

Find wood cleaner.

Clean table.

I was inside my head without attaching to his words.

His words were muffled like he had a mask covering his mouth
or I had headphones covering my ears.

His words became only sounds, like hail on tin;

"Plumpety, plump, plump. Plumpety, plump, plump," they
went.

Crunch he ate. "Plumpety, plump, plump," he spoke.

At his feet on the floor Jordan drummed a spoon on an empty
Horlicks tin.

Badum tish, Badum tish.

Mia was suckling at my breasts, *k-ah, k-ah, grrup.*

"Plumpety, plump, plump."

Badum tish, Badum tish,

K-ah, k-ah, grrup,

"Plumpety, plump, plump."

Badum tish, Badum tish

K-ah, k-ah, grrup.

Crunch, crunch.

I remember yelling "Stop!" afraid my head would explode.

He pulled his writing table away from the window and pushed
it against an empty wall.

No roofs and no birds to look at.

No roofs and no birds to talk of.

He deleted words from his sentences.

Sentences got deleted from his speech.

Like a desert waiting for a gem of water, now I thirst for him
    to speak.
I crave to hear his words, big, round and square, I wait for his
    Adam's apple to dance.
I crave to migrate with birds, paint mehndi on a hand and
    grieve for someone unknown again.

Some days he has more words than others.

Even then he is cautious.

On days he has no words at all,

I read the words on the back of the Woolworths docket:

Occidentalism.

Orientalism.

Hybridity.

Postcolonialism.

Then,

I attempt to make sense of the *Plumpety, plump, plumps* I had
    once heard.

Transform the sounds,

Make them words.

A Darn Good Cuppa

Susanna Smith

"If you're going to come down this way, you'll have to appreciate how things are 'round here," Bill said, as I sat in the passenger seat of his yellow Ford Fairmont. "We eat good tucker, and by that, I mean meat and vegetables, not foreign rubbish; we like football, and if you don't know much about footy 'round here, you'll have nothing to talk to people about; and we like a good cuppa. I like mine with a splash of real milk, none of that skinny stuff, and half a teaspoon of sugar."

Bill is my dad's best friend who also happens to be his brother-in-law, and for most of my life, I've considered him gruff, opinionated and somewhat enigmatic. When my sisters and I were kids, he'd rebuke any of our childish behaviour with a swift, sharp: "Cut that out now!" So I'd become accustomed to giving him a wide berth.

As we drove through town, I noticed not much had changed in the decades since I'd visited – the same row of shops stared blankly into the distance; the same gun-toting Ned Kelly silhouettes leaned menacingly from shop awnings, and the same galahs screeched as they circled parched paddocks in search of grain. Out at the station, the raised timber homestead still stood, oasis-like, in the middle of nowhere – shut off from the flat, deep red earth by a grove of fruit trees and a carefully tended lawn.

I'd been sceptical about my dad's decision to move to the Riverina after selling his house in Sydney. I felt that his diagnosis with Parkinson's disease made him vulnerable and I wanted him to remain close to my daughter and me. But after I'd spent a few days watching him play cards with his new-found friends and enjoy time with Bill, I knew he'd found the sense of community he'd been missing in the city. So I felt confident as I said goodbye. I told him I was going to the Australian Open in Melbourne in a few weeks and would come up and see him after that.

"You should take Bill with you," he said.

"I'd like that," Bill said.

And just like that, my visit to Melbourne became a bonding session with Uncle Bill.

* * *

"What's this rubbish?" Bill said, pushing aside the poached eggs dusted in truffle shavings with a sliver of sourdough toast he'd been served on a wooden board. "All I wanted was a good cuppa and some breakfast!"

His words ricocheted off the industrial minimalist interior of the Melbourne café and reached the waiter, who frowned and pursed his lips as he placed a pot of oolong tea and a small jug of organic milk in front of us. I'd suggested the café as an alternative to the bistro Bill usually went to. I thought he'd like coffee that you didn't have to pour yourself from a plastic urn, and eggs that weren't precooked and served from a bain-marie, but I was mistaken.

"Is this how you spend your money? What's wrong with the other place? It's good tucker!"

I shrugged and sipped my coffee.

"I like it here," I said.

I'd tried to remain open-minded about spending time with him, but all it seemed to do was magnify the differences between us.

Bill found the Australian Open challenging from the moment we arrived. He complained about the crowds and steep stairs, so once we sat down I turned the conversation to the upcoming match: Djokovic versus Federer on centre court.

"Hmmm," he said, "I don't like that bloke."

"Which bloke?"

"That Djokovic. I was listening to the radio the other day and they said the Serbs started the First World War."

"The causes of the war were more complex than that –" I said, before he cut me off.

"Why would they say something that wasn't true?" he said, glaring at me over his glasses.

"Because they can," I said.

"Stop shouting, I can't stand it," he snapped. I would, in time, come to realise that this meant Bill was wearing his hearing aid. If he wasn't, he'd urge me to "speak up".

The match was close and intense, and the crowd rose and fell and roared around us like a king tide until the early hours of the morning, when Djokovic emerged victorious. And throughout the night, Bill sat there with his arms crossed and his hands tucked under his armpits, weathering it all. "I'd have had a better view on TV," he said. "I won't be coming here again."

After the trip to Melbourne, I was hesitant to stay at Bill's, but sometimes it was the only practical option, as I had to carry things back and forth from town for my dad. And during these evenings, I developed a routine; we'd eat Bill's good tucker, I'd attempt to make a good cuppa, and I'd watch him write in a large navy blue page-to-a-day Collins diary with his left hand bent at an awkward angle as he recorded the facts about the day – rainfall, number of sheep shorn, who'd visited and where he'd been. Once he saw me watching him and mentioned he'd been forced to write with his right hand as a child. "That was at a Catholic school," he said. "The nuns knew I wasn't Catholic so they treated me terribly. I didn't last long there. We moved around so much I didn't last long at any school. As soon as I'd make friends and join the cricket team, we'd be off again."

And we'd inevitably engage in some sort of debate. I discovered Bill's bugbears pretty quickly. War, politics and religion were dominating the headlines at the time, so his general distrust of foreigners had been sharpened into particular dislikes.

"It's not right to tar everyone with the same brush," I said. But he was unperturbed.

And technology frustrated him. He'd become agitated when he called the bank or a service provider who'd send him to their website. "I don't have a computer or this internet thing," he said. "I've been running this place successfully without all of that for years and it works, why should I change it now?" When I suggested that technology could help him to be more connected to the world, he got up and pointed a remote control at his smart TV.

"Look at that," he said, pointing at the black pixelated patches that travelled across the screen, interrupting the digital transmission of an ad for crop fertiliser. "You call that better? My TV reception's never been worse! I can't even watch the footy anymore. Things were fine the way they were. Don't fix what's not broken!"

* * *

The more time I spent with my dad and Bill, the more I came to understand just how important their friendship was to one another. On one of my visits, my dad refused to eat or cooperate with his carers and he took his anger out on me when I couldn't fix the remote control he'd dropped on the floor multiple times.

"I'll talk to him," Bill said. "You go make us a cuppa."

He handed me a jar half full of teabags with a sticky label on the front with "keep out of reach of children" printed along the bottom, and "Bill and Ron's teabags" written on it in Bill's distinct handwriting. I made tea and left them to chat and when Bill encouraged Dad to eat, he didn't resist.

"Thank you," I said.

"That's fine," Bill said. "We've been friends for a long time. I've been there for him and he's been there for me. That's what friendship's all about. And that was a darn good cuppa you made for us, you've really mastered the art."

Later that night, Bill told me how he'd met my dad. "I was tired of the bush, so I thought I'd go and try my luck in

Sydney," he said. "I thought I'd play a bit of rugby and join the surf club, and that's where I met Ron, the North Bondi Surf Club. I became part of his social circle and we'd go out dancing in the city and all over town. I got to know his sister, Jann, and we were happily married for the rest of her life. It was the best thing that ever happened to me." I imagined their smiling faces and their Brylcreemed hair parted on the side as they headed out into the night in their best threads.

While I managed to perfect the cuppa and enjoyed Bill's good tucker, I never did get into the footy, but Dad did. On one visit I arrived to find out he'd beaten all the diehard Geelong Cats supporters in town to win the annual tipping competition. "How'd you manage that?" I asked as he sat there holding an envelope brimming with his cash winnings.

"Like everything," he said, "rational thinking and an educated guess."

* * *

As my dad's health deteriorated, my visits to him became more difficult. Every time I saw him, he was thinner, until his once-powerful body weighed half what mine did. He was uncooperative with his carers and I had to listen to their concerns about him and his complaints about them, while dealing with my own sense of impending loss. At the end of those days, I drove out into the blackness of the unlit road and relished the silence. I'd scan the road ahead for the kangaroos who'd bound into my path and slow right down and follow them until they disappeared back into the night. I'd count the creeks as I crossed them – Billabong, Turn Back Jimmy, Yanco

– to gauge where I was until I saw the glint of the farm entrance sign and felt the vibration of the cattle grids under the tyres as I arrived at the station. And when I got to the house, Bill would have a fire going and dinner ready – roast lamb and potatoes, and his homemade bread and butter pudding.

One night I noticed a schedule of Uniting Church services on his fridge with dates and times underlined in blue pen. I'd never heard him talk about his religious beliefs, so I asked him if he'd been going to church. "Sometimes," he said. "I've always had this ability to know when something was wrong out on the land, and so many times I've followed that feeling and something has been wrong – one of my animals was in trouble or something else was up – and it made me think that there was someone up there lookin' out for me."

* * *

Five years after Dad left Sydney, he lost his battle with Parkinson's disease. Bill was the first person to call me. "Yeahh," he said. It was all he could say and all that needed to be said. He took care of everything for me. And when I collected my dad's belongings, I found the jar of teabags that he and Bill had shared for all those years and took it home as a memento of unconditional friendship.

I found it hard to return to the Riverina again after my dad died, as if the place embodied a painful absence – the only café in town reminded me of his fondness for pizza and the local supermarket of his specific request for bananas that were just a little bit green – and so my contact with Bill became sporadic. But one night he called me out of the blue.

"G'day," he said, before giving me his usual rundown: how much rainfall he'd had, how many rams he'd sold and how the dogs were doing.

"How are you?" I asked.

"I've been doin' great," he said. "I've been selling lots of wool to that bloke."

"Which bloke?"

"You know, that one in North Korea."

"Kim Jong-un?"

"Yeah, that bloke."

"So we're trading with North Korea now?" I asked, as his chuckling let me know I'd been had.

"But I really wanted to tell you about something that happened to me," he said.

He told me he'd gone down to Melbourne to get his eyes tested and he was on a crowded tram, hanging on for dear life, when he felt a gentle touch on his elbow guide him toward a vacant seat.

"It was a little Muslim girl," he said, "and it completely changed me. A complete change, isn't that amazing? I thought you'd want to know."

"That's great, Bill," I said, "that's amazing."

While Bill could adapt his attitudes toward some things, he remained less accommodating about others. I realised this when I called him to thank him for a letter he'd sent written on a Commonwealth Bank envelope containing a fifty-dollar note with the message: "Have a cup of tea on me. B!"

"Who?" he yelled when he answered.

"Susanna," I yelled back.

"I can't hear you."

"Ron's daughter."

"Naaaah," he said. "Where're you from?"

"Sydney."

"I can't hear you."

I hung up. I assumed he'd either refused to put on his hearing aid, or his landline connection was damaged – possibly both. And for a split second, I wondered if I could send him a text, but I knew it was pointless. When it came to technology he remained stubbornly isolated on the other side of the digital divide. And he wouldn't have it any other way.

walking to a babysitting job, 28/5/22

Zoe Morris

Look! Up there,
bursting out of the golden sky like a pealing bell,
like a trumpet call,
a rainbow!
She zooms over the old sandstone
of the nursing home
where the prismatic lorikeets play.
Darling, I noticed them first,
so the rainbow
felt like a wink from God.

I feed blueberries to the baby with my bare hands.
She hugs my hip,
she pulls my hair,
and I think of the way the world
sings to us each day,
for pure joy and without payment.
Today, perhaps she was singing to me
and her payment was the way
I wanted to fling myself onto the concrete screaming,
pulling my hair out, crying, like a new convert.

So full of love my heart was pounding out of my skin
and had become part of the sky.

Sky blue like beaches.
Sky orange like the summer sun.
Sky billowing and blowing
coral behind the neck of a mandarin tree.
Sky raining yellow like I'm Danaë.
Sky purple,
sky pink,
sky sweet as peaches.

The baby cries. Eventually
she falls asleep, and
I leave surrounded by black velvet
and silver berries.
I open my mouth wide
and taste holy wine.

Neighbourhood Wisteria

Emma Murphy

Wisteria settles
throughout the neighbourhood
as shining leaves shimmer
under peppering sunlight,
and lilac petals
turn into hummingbird wings.

My arms stack on top of each other
like books
and my mind outruns
the bus I am on,
distracted by the world
in front of me.

My eyes absorb
melting brooks at the end
of a winter's solstice,
and tall trees
that dance in the
whispers of the wind.

I settle for the charms
of bedroom community landscapes,
and white picket fences
concealing "welcome home"
slaughterhouses.

The wildflower cottage
ingested in ivy
on the corner of the woodlands
resides in fairy tales
and in a life that is not
mine,

but I hope, someday,
it can be.

Happiness in the Steel Strings

Wooden Peach

*This poem is dedicated to the great songwriter, Nobel Prize
winner, my icon, Bob Dylan.*

Years ago, I heard a folk song,
The melody spiralled in my heart for so long.
From then on, I fell in love with folk music,
And I got my guitar, which was steel-stringed acoustic.

The six amazing and mysterious strings,
Always wiped my sorrow into the wind.
Whenever I played the different chords,
I was immersed in the music and got lost.

My guitar has brought me to many places –
To Scarborough, to see the tears on girls' faces;
To Greenwich, to see the 500-mile journey of Davis;
To Virginia, the country road has been there for ages.

I try to seek happiness in everyday life;
Inside the guitar, the pleasure shines.
The happiness is in the six steel strings,
Now and forever, I will sing.

Presence

Harold Legaspi

The splendour of the horizon made a lasting impression on Lee, who was hosting a birthday *fiesta* in the Blue Mountains. In the open air, the jewelled sun rose beyond the stratosphere. Old relatives sat, legs crossed like bows, listening to a niece propose a toast. A farewell bid to the bygone eras, Lee humbly bowed his head, then took his place beside his partner.

A nihilistic, testosterone-fuelled twenties, followed by arresting contemplation in his thirties, and resplendent awakening in his forties meant that now, in his fifties, anything was possible. Lately, his somewhat meek existence had been spoken of by his relatives. It cast shadows among the flowers, the bees, the skies and the seas. Relatives, among them, his precious aunts, never failed to shower him with hard knocks and praises, which brought him glee, knowing he was spoken of in hisses and hoots.

He shied away from his conundrums by expressing his gratitude towards his guests. He had been dreaming of days to come, leaping over moons. His tongue, flowing with reverie, called upon a sense of duty to mention those who had helped him build his home.

His nieces and nephews looked upon the sky, blessed by the elegant flight of a dove, released by his father. The mood elevated: piñatas smashed, confetti thrown – a livening of spirits.

Music roared from the radio as guests dwindled in harmonious rhythm. The atmosphere tinted with hues, pinks and blues, softened, till he and his partner were the only ones remaining. Lee whispered in his partner's ear, and with virtue and longing, cradled him before making their way back home. He bathed in the pureness of innocent love, as he shushed his partner into a drowsy spirit, shot with languid affection. Back at home, Lee unwrapped his partner's gift. Bejewelled! Spirited! Dazzling! Transcendent!

A Room Without Books

Tom Evans

It's always a bittersweet feeling going back to the home where you grew up. Be it out of duty, guilt, sadness or even love, home is what we make of it.

Away from the noise, the sprawl of apartment blocks and traffic jams and sirens and people and people and people. The refuge of the suburbs offers the promise of calm, a tapestry of greens and ochre, bricks and corrugated roofs. Even the air is cleaner, cars are but a distant drone, drowned out by birds calling, dogs barking, and sputtering lawnmowers.

This is what coming home is. Monday to Friday, the nine-to-five, all these anxieties evaporate once the steam from the kettle on a gas stove whistles out and Mum is there to pour me a cup of tea.

A place increasingly foreign yet always so familiar. That coffee table I chipped, a stain on the carpet, plaster indents on the wall from when I got into an argument with my brother . . . It's like an exhibition of your life that you pay for in emotional time.

When my dog limps over to me and looks up with her grey hairs and cloudy eyes, I still pat her the same way that I did for all those years when I was younger. Mum smiles as the conversation starts to flow, so refreshingly honest that I sit back on the faded leather couch and listen as my tea gets cold on that battered coffee table.

Once the conversation stills and the teapot is emptied, it's time to say my goodbyes and venture back into the outside world, back to a new life. Sometimes this moment brings relief, other times a feeling you can't get out of your throat. It's always the same, the ritual.

* * *

I arrive late one Friday night, exhausted after a stressful week at work. As the days get colder and the nights get lonelier, the excitement of living alone dampens, the reality of life takes over.

Friends are now in relationships or too busy with work or study to catch up. The sanctity of Friday drinks has been threatened by other commitments. It seems as if all the fun of my early twenties is slowly receding like my hairline, the passage of time has led me down the path of full-time work and the desperation for companionship.

Swiping right on apps and braving all the first or second dates have slowly worn away at the optimism of my younger self. Will I ever find love through an app I only use when I'm drunk? Will that one true love manifest itself with "It's a match!" as we lock eyes in a dimly lit bar in the CBD? Grandma, my most fervent supporter, still tells me how handsome I am, so I know that I still have some time left before my personality needs to improve.

I've probably been on more dates this year than grandma has in her whole life, but we can't all have the Hallmark love story that every baby boomer seems to have.

Today was different though, as this was the week I finally decided that the same routine of the past years needed to change. And by divine intervention, Mum's weekly text of "How's things?" came in the middle of a meeting at work, when I needed it most. My reply was not "Yeah, good", but rather "Not the best". That set the wheels in motion.

It was only 11 am and I had not even started work for the day at my underpaid job, except for the meeting I had just dissociated from, but Mum had already sprung into action, and we texted well into lunchtime. The audible sounds that came from my stomach eventually ended the conversation and I promised that I'd stay over the weekend, something I'd never done before.

And so, here I stand – cold and in the dark on my old family home's front porch. The faded light of the lamp beside the front door and the complete stillness of this leafy suburb is unsettling at first, but as I wait for Mum to take the food off the stove, it's comforting.

Mum opens the door with a look of concern that's immediately followed by a crushing hug. She smells of garlic, onions and a hint of smoke from the fire she started earlier.

Led into the living room with a roaring fire and greeted by our Cocker Spaniel who now suffers from arthritis, I rub her in the same spot behind her right ear that I know she likes the most, even after all these years.

I tell Mum about trips planned with friends and a hopeful promotion at work. As the bottles empty and the night wears on, my little brother emerges from upstairs and rushes out the door, leaving it to the last minute exactly like he did when we used to live in adjacent rooms.

When the final bottle of Pinot Noir is finished and the conversation dies down, I attempt to flick through the free-to-air channels, but it becomes an endless scroll. I yawn and stretch my arms, standing up to go upstairs to my old bedroom. It's been over two years since I've slept in my old room. Usually, a moment like this would lead to the jangling of keys and hugs goodbye. But now, it's just sort of an awkward "Goodnight" and off to bed.

Even in darkness, I still remember where the light switches are on the way upstairs and down the hallway to my bedroom. In my old room, I flick the switch and the room is illuminated by a dim yellow light I never got around to replacing.

I breathe deeply now, not used to feeling out of place in a room I had spent most of my life in. It's so dark and quiet, completely different to the city apartment I live in now, above a major road with blinds that don't close properly.

The "guest room" is the best way to describe my room now, stripped bare of its old contents. All the furniture is still in the right place, but it doesn't feel quite right, this doesn't feel like home.

I turn to my side, rubbing my hand through my hair until I realise that my bookshelf running across the back wall is still there as I had left it. A collection of paperbacks and special signed copies built up over the years that are the clearest expression of me.

This bookshelf is a timeline, starting from bottom with the junior fiction and fantasy series I read as a kid, bruised and battered from the late nights reading under the covers while Mum thought I was asleep. They now sit flush against the bottom shelves as I run my fingers over the spines and look up to the classics that sit in the middle.

My high school days where I read nonstop but still felt insecure that I hadn't read Camus or Dickens, so I dragged Mum to the local bookshop to fill my shelves. While some of these classics remain among my most cherished, most have sat idle for over a decade on this shelf as I haven't found the time or motivation to read them since. A second-hand copy of *Anna Karenina* is shoved between other books by great Russian writers, the cracked spines and browning pages only passed on to me, not read.

Then, I arrive at the contemporary novels on the top shelves, the memoirs and non-fiction and prize winners that I still think back to or still borrow on my brief trips home. George Saunders, Ali Smith, Siri Hustvedt, an assortment of colours and sizes that all inspired me in unique ways. On a train trip to work, by the pool one summer, even curled up in my single bed that was too small for me late at night. Gifts from a past girlfriend, from Mum or a friend or just for myself, these books are who I am or who I want to be.

I pick up a copy of *Congratulations, By the Way* by George Saunders from the shelf, only a thin book barely visible on the shelf, but with so much meaning to me. I first read it on a holiday three years ago backpacking around Europe; the words captured my imagination and still cause me to stop and think about the importance of living in the present. Each spine tells its own story of a moment in my life, of love, hope, and sadness. Before I moved out, I had finally filled this bookshelf with a collection of me, each piece of the puzzle with its own place on the shelf.

Standing back, biting my bottom lip with my hands resting on my hips, I feel a warmth I haven't felt in a long time. The knot in my stomach seems to untangle as I look over each and every spine on the shelf. But, the knot returns when I notice a gap on the top shelf.

There is a book missing and one that must have meant a lot to me, but I can't tell which one it was. I've reached the point where there are so many books read or purchased that titles and authors tend to lose meaning. Instead, the books that stick with me become a feeling or experience. The name of this book escapes me but I remember clearly reading it on a train trip around four years ago. From a poet to his mum, a love letter in beautiful prose.

Why did I even come here? There was a reason why I never stay over anymore, so many better things to do with the little free time I have these days. The refuge of my bookshelf that had promised so much tonight is slipping away from me as I turn off the light and feel suffocated by the complete darkness of the room.

* * *

Trying to fall asleep brings little success as I cling desperately to the flannel sheets of my single bed, constantly bumping my head against the wood at the top that is covered with faded stickers.

It seems strange that forgetting the name of a book would cause me to toss and turn in my old room, but as the hours pass the familiar softness of the sheets and stillness of the leafy suburb makes me breathe deeply. Away from the drones of cars and artificial lights of my apartment in the city, the total darkness of my family home covers me like a weighted blanket. Familiar and welcoming, the flannel sheets now make me feel at ease and I fall into a deep sleep.

I wake up refreshed and go downstairs to make scrambled eggs the way I always made them before I moved out, but haven't since. The worries of the previous weeks at work seem to fade away as I sit down at the wooden table in the kitchen, light slicing through the leaves outside and warming my skin. There is an energy in this room I cannot describe, for the first time in years I feel satisfied.

Impatient as always, I decide to walk down the road to the shops by myself and explore what has become of a place I frequented every weekend in a past life.

Saturday morning. The once quiet village I knew growing up is now alive with activity. Lines at new cafés, children running around giggling and free, couples of all ages holding hands. This is a sight I am unused to living in the CBD where everyone's lives seem to be waiting for something more important – rushing down grocery aisles, talking on the phone intensely while waiting for a coffee. Even the kids that parents hurriedly lead into apartment foyers and off the busy streets.

Although there are families with kids and older couples enjoying themselves and taking things slow, which is great to see, all the shops I grew up with and remember so fondly are now gone, including the bookshop.

From a shy kid starting kindergarten to a more assured adult finishing university, the local bookshop meant, and will always mean, so much to me. Like my bookshelf in my old room, the bookshop was an extension of me. I could be myself in the quiet and peaceful aisles of that thin and long building. Those countless times I walked through those sliding doors and was greeted by a beaming smile from the older woman behind the counter was a simple pleasure.

Now, as I walk past the sliding doors that now open to the foyer of a tutorial college, I feel indifferent. Only when I look up and see the awning of the bookshop rusted with chipping paint do I clench my hand and cross the road to the supermarket. Time to go home.

Instead, I come across a new store that I haven't seen before. I can't remember what stood here before – probably a massage parlour – but now I am greeted by a tub of books with a hand-drawn sign:

Bargain Books for only $2!

With feigned interest, I walk into this new second-hand bookshop with low expectations, expecting a disinterested young person leaving messy shelves of genre novels no one reads and cookbooks no one can decipher.

An old lady carefully rearranging the shelves smiles at me, catching me off guard with this feeling of being welcomed and safe.

The shelves around me house the usual crime and romance novels that I've never known anyone to read besides my grandma. I pick up some older books I recognise, curious but put off by the cracked spines and ripped pages. Turning over the tattered covers, I think about the previous lives each book has had. Was this contemporary romance once a gift, this memoir an impulse buy, this poetry book from someone desperately in love? Maybe I should buy this one, but I haven't enjoyed a poem in years.

Sighing, I bend down and put the book back on the shelf before noticing a familiar spine on one of the bottom shelves. Between the cracked spines from an old crime writer is one of my favourite books in seemingly perfect condition.

Running my finger along the book before taking it off the shelf, I realise that this is the book that was missing from my bookshelf at home. It seems strange that a book that meant so much to me was forgotten until now, that the title and author escaped me but the feelings it captured for me were always there. Inside the front flap of the dust jacket is the same sticker from my old bookshop, in the same spot as the copy I had lost, and it is still in perfect condition. *On Earth We're Briefly Gorgeous* by Ocean Vuong, the name now clear to see.

This doesn't make any sense. I have never given away any of my books and Mum would never do so, but this copy feels exactly as I remember my own. I flick through the pages, desperate to find any indication that this is my own copy – any tabs, pencilled notes, or even dog-eared pages. Nothing except for a folded receipt tucked into the back pages.

With shallow breaths I unfold the receipt, only to see that the text has almost completely faded as all ink on old receipts slowly does. Straining under the fluorescent light of the shop to see, I can just make out a date, 2019. Or is it 2020? No, the store closed at the end of 2019 so it must be the right year, but I can't make out which month or day. I fold the receipt and put it in my pocket, something to hold on to regardless.

Clutching the book with both hands and walking up to the girl behind the counter, I think of all the times in years gone past where a book like this gave me hope, gave me meaning. Perhaps this decision to go home was not in vain, perhaps it is an opportunity to remember. Our pasts are a part of who we are today, and it is time to cherish the present.

"That will be five dollars please," says the girl behind the counter, with whom I'm too nervous to make eye contact.

Not out of fear, but uncertainty. This is a book I found at a second-hand bookstore, and yet handing it over to someone feels like I am handing over a piece of myself. It feels like giving away my secrets, laying bare all of me through a hardcover book with a dust jacket wrapped around it.

"Oh my God! This is one of my favourite books! Where did you find this?"

"I didn't think anyone could like this book as much as I did. It was hidden away in that corner among the faded copies of Wilbur Smith and James Patterson," I say, pointing to the corner of the shop behind me.

"That's so cool," she says. "I remember when I first read this book, I'd be in tears at the end of each chapter. Don't you love how books can be so meaningful like that?"

I stare at her blankly, thinking about last night and the weeks gone by. The connections with books and people, going home to what was familiar, and being comforted by the little things that I took for granted when I was younger.

There is no way to capture the wags of a dog's tail or the smell of tea brewing from Mum's teapot when I return home to my apartment alone. But what I can bring back with me is this book now nestled in my arms. It will find a home in my room on my new bookshelf, a place not as big or meaningful as the one in my childhood home, but one that I will slowly build up again. A room with books.

An Ordinary Evening at Ashgrove

Blake Isaac Falcongreen

For my sisters

Don't think about all the things that are terrible.
Let them pass through your mind like stowaways.
   Let them drop past your eyes like vertigo.

Dream of summertime swimming at the pool by
your house, of the sizzling concrete and sunscreen
   smells, of the red-eyed magpies who fly from the sun.

Dream of the straw-yellow hills of endless suburbia
that you rolled your bike down, the neighbour's house
   you weren't allowed to go near, or the shrill

shrieking from across the road – the other small
silences of the night, that lulled you to sleep those
   years ago, that you held tightly until morning.

Remember the underground room adjoining your bed,
the creepy cockroach bombs that lined the floor
   like space saucers, the awkward trail of ants

along the white brick walls, the cat's shallow grave
and the hazy yellow memory around it. Think about
the pale-fisted wails rising from the

nearby bedrooms, or the eroding creek line by the
mulberries, or the sanctity of your locked door, and
watch them run past your vision like fiction.

Stepping Out for Air

Sophie Bellotti

You wake up and it's a day like any other. Except not
really: today is *now*. Today is *happening*. Time
passes in the idiosyncratic manner of the thing we call
the present, continuous, with its potential
for anything and everything. Today is the day you have
to live through – simple as that.

At times the smallest things make it easy:
some satisfying syntax; your lover's eyelash. Other days,
the opposite. The past has a proclivity for distension and
compression. Spend long enough gazing back
and time becomes the tube of a telescope, zeroing in
till an instant becomes larger than life.
Spend too much time at either end of the viewfinder,
you're asking for trouble. You risk losing the moment
to memory. Your day-to-day is a flimsy mount,
supporting a tool of distortion.

You go out to reaffirm your boundaries. Moving
through the community: no one here
knows your name. Yet someone waves

from behind the dark tint of a windscreen. The intimacy
in the way they anticipate your next move. Awareness
of the other's presence, passing bodies in space.
You stop traffic; you are a shape.

Your feet meet the asphalt, shifting
rocks. In Sydney, it's necessary to watch the ground
for cockroaches, especially
as the sky begins to darken. You lose your ability
to walk straight when you look up. On a particularly clouded
    day,
you can always point to that colour of dusk, the muting
of shades you tend to associate with melancholy,
and state, This is a beautiful time
for light. You intervene
in the trajectory of ants. How many times you've changed
the course of a life.

Today you really notice the flowers – portents
of a hotter future, affirming that
we're all born dying. The man in high vis
who sits facing the street with a schooner
every afternoon, sometimes with a friend, more often
alone. You are the same – drawing
outlines around yourselves; affirming your perimeters
through contextual clues. Held

here, if only momentarily. But solid; not nebulous
and liable to evaporate, the way you cease to be
when you squint into a mirror from a reasonable distance.

A Life of Moments

Aoife Edwards

Freya loved these moments.

In fact, she was quite sure she loved them more than any other moments in her life. She wanted to resent her mother for claiming her favourite memories, when these days she often featured so poorly in all the others – and yet Freya could not stop herself from loving them.

The cobblestone street in The Rocks curved away up ahead. White stalls lined either side of the road, vendors tending to wares of every kind: sizzling Italian cuisine, tinkling music boxes, handmade fudge, children's toys, tea leaves, and leather bags, all Australiana themed.

Music wound around the gentle flow of people. Warm sunlight stretched down from the open blue sky.

Freya and her mother sat at the Tea Cosy. It was a quaint, successful establishment right at the wide-open corner of The Rocks Markets. It was perfectly positioned to make the most of a wide selection of outdoor seating and views of the beloved markets, and even the Harbour in the distance.

A wicker basket filled with thick woollen thread and knitting needles added a splash of colour to every table. Freya's chair even had a pink, blue and white crocheted blanket folded over the back.

Freya finally looked at her mother.

In these moments, her mother always seemed more . . . peaceful? Content? Distracted? It was hard to place. But she wasn't overwhelmed by busy days, or the never-ending demand for new and interesting dinner ideas, or the all-consuming concern for her children's future.

Somehow, in these moments, the tension abated and a soothing contentment filled the empty space.

If Freya were to try painting this scene, she would struggle with which colours to use – bold cool tones to reflect the joy and busyness of the scene, or warm soft pastels to reflect the peace at the heart of it all?

"Long black?" a sweet voice prompted.

"Here," Freya's mother said, smiling brightly at the waitress as she unloaded her tray.

"And the cappuccino for you," the waitress murmured, placing a mug the size of a small bowl in front of Freya.

She also set down a pale wicker basket of two thick white scones, two pots of gleaming blackberry jam and fluffy cream.

"The size of these mugs never fails to shock me." Her mother shook her head, smiling.

Freya smiled, lifting the mug to her lips using two hands, one wrapped around the smooth varnished handle and the fingertips of her other hand poised on the opposite side.

The mugs *were* huge, shining with varnish and multicoloured pastels. You would think that all the colours in the café would clash, but somehow the spacious sprawl of tables allowed for the many splashes of colour without seeming overwhelming.

With her first creamy sip of coffee, Freya sighed. She looked out to the markets once again.

"Do you think Ricky will ever go back to uni?" her mother asked.

She didn't sound upset – another magical feature of this place. It somehow made all worries seem smaller.

"Probably," Freya replied, clasping her mug in her hands and resting it against her chest. "But if he doesn't, it'll be because he's found something more worthwhile. Something he wants to work at."

Her heart swelled, hoping that her mother would remember those words next time she spoke with Ricky. There were two kinds of concern – helpful and unhelpful. Helpful concern would have been telling your son that you love him, and that you are sure he will find the right path if he keeps working hard. Unhelpful concern was insisting that he needs to complete his university degree while he is still young, because that is the only path a successful child can take. The most important thing, of course, is that both kinds have the best of intentions – and intention is largely irrelevant.

"Ready for your scone?" Freya asked, dragging her wandering mind from its reverie.

"Of *course*."

They both cut into the fluffy, crumbling dough and slathered it with gooey blackberry jam before piling it with smooth cream. The first bite had Freya moaning.

"I've missed these. So much."

"Mmmm," was all her mother said, too focused on the scone in her hand.

"You know, I was telling Maria about this place."

"Oh! When did you see her?"

"Friday; we went into the city for brunch and book shopping."

"That sounds so lovely. Has she ever been here?"

A twinge of reality crept in. Freya knew that if they were talking about Theo instead of Maria, the conversation would have stilted.

"Oh? Has he ever been here?" her mother would have said.

"No, but I'm dying to bring him."

And it would have ended there.

But Freya did not want to think about that. Because moments like this were lovely and you hold onto lovely moments in the not-so-lovely moments. As long as moments like this existed, they would out-live the not-so-lovely ones.

* * *

Freya and her mother carefully chose a table with plush comfortable chairs that was usually occupied. On a rainy day like this, they had an opportunity to dine in unexpected comfort.

It was a good sign. And Freya needed a good sign today.

They ordered their usual coffees and scones and sat and waited.

The wet drizzle had threatened many of the usual vendors. Half the stalls weren't set up today, and the few that were open struggled to attract the attention of passers-by hurrying into the nearest pubs or indoor venues.

There was no music either.

Freya tried to appreciate the day as it was. The cool breeze rustled her warm hoodie, and the smell of rain had her sitting and sniffing, just inhaling the scent she couldn't get enough of.

The chair was comfy and the coffee was hot and the scones were sweet. The rain was soft and the day was quiet and so too was her mother.

Too quiet.

The tension hung between them, taunting each into a silence neither wanted to break. Her mother bit the bullet first.

"I don't want things to be like this between us," she said, setting her coffee down and looking out to the dreary sky.

"Me neither. But I don't think going over it again will help."

Freya wished she had the right words to soothe her mother. She had *some* words in her mind – words that would indeed alleviate her mother's fear and anger and loss. But to say them would be a betrayal to herself. Was she selfish for not prioritising her mother? Of course she loved her. Of course she wanted peace between them. But some iron-willed throbbing in her chest locked those words away deep inside her.

It wasn't a matter of pride. Freya was used to putting aside her pride, apologising and recognising her errors. She did it frequently, because she had a tendency to be quite thoughtless. Well-intentioned, but thoughtless nonetheless.

But she couldn't make promises that betrayed the deepest desires of her heart, desires that she had kept locked away for years. Now that someone had unlocked them and set them free, she couldn't put them back no matter the chaos they had birthed.

She had never been so happy and so distraught at the same time.

"So, what? This is just how we're going to be from now on?"

Freya tried to breathe through the note of accusation in her mother's voice. *Good intentions. She loves me. She is scared.*

"No, of course not. We just have to . . . find a new way."

Her mother was quiet.

She looked again at the grey day and couldn't help feeling it was reflecting her mood. The photographer started packing his shots of the Australian ocean and desert into boxes.

* * *

Freya loved her balcony. It had to be the most beloved part of her new apartment.

"I'm going to work, love. I love you," Theo said, one hand on the back of her neck as he kissed her forehead.

"Love you," she called after him.

"Hey." His head popped into the visible doorframe once again. "Make sure you rest this morning, okay? Leave the kitchen for me."

Her smile was warm.

"I'll think about it."

"I'm serious," he said with a warning look.

The door clicked shut behind him.

She took a deep breath in through her nose and let it out through her mouth. She remembered a yoga instructor once calling it a "deep cleansing breath", and the name had stuck with her because she couldn't deny its accuracy.

The balcony railing was a perfect height. High enough to provide privacy when sitting down, but low enough to allow a view over the sprawling park beyond, with its lush grass and scattered trees that towered over the apartment.

Their balcony furniture had been a snatch, too – a bench lounge, two armchairs and a table, for hundreds of dollars cheaper than expected just because two unnoticeable bamboo pieces were snapped.

She was undeniably proud of her balcony space. It had clean bamboo furniture, soft white seating and plush blue cushions. A glass top table held three individually potted succulents in pots of blue, white, and pink. A thriving fern sat in the corner, adding a refreshing touch to the space.

It wasn't . . . fancy. But it was comfortable and colourful and clean and lovely. She came out here all the time, be it summer or winter. In summer, she brought out iced teas and novels. In winter, she had coffee and online classes.

Whenever the mornings would allow, she would sit with her breakfast and watch the quiet park. She would get lost in thought and start her days with beauty and peace.

She also frequently found herself looking at the armchair beside her and feeling her heart throb a bit. In those moments, the day lost its lustre and her coffee lost its richness. She became a bit too cold to sit outside, a bit too busy. There were things she needed to do.

Freya looked at the fern, its deep green leaves reaching as far as they could, forever striving to grow bigger and bigger.

She looked at the park and felt the cool breeze on her cheeks. She breathed in the quiet.

She looked at the mug on the glass tabletop. Soft stoneware, pastel blue. Empty now, its sides stained with foam and dried coffee.

Time to go.

There were things to do.

* * *

Julianna had a difficult relationship with being busy.

When she was busy, as she often was, she resented the lack of rest. She wished to lie down and watch a good movie. She wished to soak in a hot bubbly lavender-scented bath. She wished for the freedom and energy to exercise or see a friend.

When she was not busy, as she sometimes was . . . well, it was like a constant itch. An itch in her toes to get up and move. An itch in her hands to make or do or fix. An itch in her mind to jump from one thought to another to another.

And when she was forced to rest, she resented the lack of peace in her mind preventing her from truly enjoying it.

There was a perfect middle ground she was constantly trying to balance. The perfect amount of noise and business to keep her moving, without being so noisy and so busy as to make her tired and overwhelmed, with a little bit of rest in the evenings.

It was evening in Sydney now. This meant Julianna was curled up on the couch with her feet tucked under her, her current Netflix series catching her attention with its small-town drama.

Evening in Sydney also meant it was morning in Edinburgh. Ricky was in Edinburgh. Julianna wondered what he was doing now. Studying, probably. But had he forgotten his breakfast again? Had he slept in too much, as he always did? She was certain he had not washed his clothes in at least two weeks. He was accustomed to letting a month go by before the smell reminded him that his small studio apartment had a free-to-use laundry downstairs.

Her heart ached to be near him. She wished he were just close *by*, so that if something happened – if he needed her – she would not be half a world away.

But she had visited a mere month ago. He was deep in the throes of exams now and didn't need any distractions. Or loving mothers.

Her fingers itched. She thought of the empty bucket beside the fireplace that her husband had promised to fill in the morning.

She paused her show, stood up from the couch, slipped on her thongs and some thick rubber gloves. She grabbed the bucket and went to fill it with thick logs of wood from the large stack outside.

She lugged the bucket back in, cursing, and dropped it by the fireplace. There was a small crackling fire warming the house, but it would slowly die while they slept through the night. Unless her husband, as he sometimes did, woke up in the early hours of the morning to tend to it and keep it burning.

She sat on the edge of the nearest couch, pulled off the thick gloves and warmed her hands.

Her phone pinged the moment she sat down.

She cursed quietly, stood up and went back to her television-watching position.

After she had tucked her feet under the blanket, she looked at the phone.

A text from Freya.

Whatcha doing tomorrow morning?

Appointment at 11.30. Nothing before that.

Want to go into The Rocks?

Julianna's heart skipped a beat. Her blood hummed.

Tomorrow is probably a bit tight . . . what about Wednesday?

Perfect :)

They were going out for coffee. They hadn't been into The Rocks in nearly a year.

Julianna immediately went into the kitchen and wrote it onto her calendar.

FREYA COFFEE.

She let out a shaky breath. She was nervous and excited and hopeful and hurt.

Her mind itched.

She went back to the lounge. She pressed play on her show and lost herself in the small-town drama: the schoolteacher, her troubled pupils and her noble officer love.

* * *

Julianna strode through the cobblestone streets, weaving through the busy mill of people admiring the market wares.

She was early. She was always early. But she would get a table and order the coffee so it was hot and ready when Freya arrived.

She caught sight of the colourful knitting baskets and blankets up ahead.

When she reached the curling iron arch that led into the outdoor seating area, she made for one of the nearby tables with two soft crocheted blankets. Summer *was* approaching but there was still a cool breeze –

"Mum!"

Despite the chatter and music and sizzling filling the air, she would recognise her children's voices anywhere.

She looked up and spotted Freya already seated in the cosy armchairs.

Early. Just like her.

She smiled and made her way over.

"You're early!" she exclaimed, giving her daughter a quick hug before settling into the armchair, dropping her bag between her feet and moving the cosy blanket to her lap.

Freya laughed.

"I can't *not* be early. It's in my DNA."

"Have you ordered yet?"

Freya nodded.

"I've known your coffee order since I could talk. I did get extra scones though 'cause I'm *starving.*"

"That's okay! What's Theo up to today?"

Freya's gaze jumped from the markets to Julianna.

"Good! Working, so he couldn't come in. I still haven't got the chance to show him the markets."

"Oh, he has to come in sometime. Take a weekend off. You can't live in Sydney and not see The Rocks Markets."

Of course, that was a family tradition, and many Sydneysiders wouldn't prioritise The Rocks Markets as one of the city's great highlights. But Julianna's family had been coming here since before they ever had children, when it was just Julianna and her husband and the Tea Cosy was barely a possibility, a thought.

Freya smiled. It was warm and hopeful and joyous.

"He does. I'm going to try make him take a day off so we can come in and see everything from The Rocks to the Botanic Gardens."

Julianna's heart warmed.

An upbeat thread of music caught her attention. She looked out into the street.

At the corner of the winding road, a man played a Spanish guitar. The warm notes bounced and swayed among the chatter.

"Beautiful, isn't it?" she murmured.

"It is! He's very good," Freya agreed.

Soon their coffee and scones arrived. The colourful mugs were big enough to require two hands, just like always, and the fluffy hot scones steamed in the cool morning air. Something inside Julianna buzzed.

Her fingers itched – only to hold the mug. When it settled between her palms and she held it close to her chest, warmth flooded through her. She took a deep breath in, and all her itching flowed out with her breath. Heavy peace settled in her limbs.

"I've missed this place," Freya admitted, shaking her head.

"Me too."

They looked out over the market and sipped their coffee and listened to the Spanish guitar until the man packed up. They ate their hot scones with gooey raspberry jam and smooth cream and enjoyed each other's presence. Sometimes they chatted about the stalls and the interesting people and Freya's unfolding career and Julianna's plans for her future. Sometimes they just sat and listened and watched and appreciated.

* * *

Julianna tried not to stare at her daughter.

She hadn't expected Freya to look *well*, not after the difficulty of the last year. But she hadn't expected this.

Freya sat in one of the bamboo chairs on her balcony, Julianna in the other. The chair wasn't overly large, but it now dwarfed Freya's thin, bony shoulders and flat stomach. Her skin was dull and her cheeks hollow and her eyes empty. Her hair lay limp over her prominent collarbone.

Julianna picked up her coffee mug and pressed it into Freya's cold hands, wrapping her fingers around the mug.

Freya tried to smile at her, but barely managed to tilt up the corner of her lips. Her eyes remained cold.

"You need to eat. I can make you some eggs if you don't want the toast."

"Not yet – just sit with me for a minute."

Julianna couldn't ignore the pleading tone in her daughter's request. Her whole body ached.

She picked up her own coffee and took a sip.

She looked out.

The balcony rail was now lined with Julianna's gift – curling iron pots filled with flowers, bursts of yellow and purple and white.

She remembered the flowers she had brought Freya in hospital, the soft pink lilies with white baby's breath and emerald leaves.

She would never forget Freya sobbing in her arms, crying and murmuring over and over that she didn't know what to do, clutching her round belly. Julianna hadn't had any advice – she couldn't. As a mother she couldn't suggest Freya terminate the baby's life to save her own, because she herself could not have done it. As *Freya's* mother, she couldn't ever suggest she go ahead with the pregnancy and risk her own life.

She blinked back the tears in her eyes and refocused on her coffee.

"Do you mind if I put some music on?" she asked her daughter.

Freya shook her head.

She chose soft melancholic jazz. The speakers oozed the flowing notes and Julianna visibly saw Freya's chest rise and fall with a deep breath.

Freya even nibbled the corner of the toast.

Julianna tried not to sob with relief. *Please God.*

* * *

"Do you remember Ricky's wedding?"

The whole family had travelled to Scotland for the affair, and what a holiday it had been. They had fallen in love with the charm of Edinburgh and scoured the city for every café and antiques store possible. They had spent a weekend in the Highlands, among the rugged mountains and rolling hills and ancient stones. They had celebrated one of the most beautiful weddings Freya had ever seen.

And yet the things Freya remembered most surprised her. She thought of dancing with Theo, spinning and swaying until her feet gave out and her body slumped into a chair. She thought of her father admiring the shadowed mountains on the horizon, a pint of cold beer sweating in the heat, clasped in his hand. She thought of the next morning, when she and her mother had been the only ones awake and they had snuck out into the gardens. They had shared steaming tea and leftover cake among the rose-scented air.

"Bits and pieces," her mother admitted. "I'll never forget the cake – I've never tasted chocolate so rich since."

They both knew it wasn't true, that she would never forget it. But neither said so. Her mother had been forgetting a lot of things recently.

"Was Lucy here this morning?"

Her mother nodded.

"She helped me shower and made me breakfast, but I told her to leave early today. It's her lovely daughter's birthday and I told her she should spend the day with family."

Lucy, her mother's carer, came five times a week in the morning to make Julianna breakfast, help her shower and take a walk, then do some house cleaning and make her mother lunch before leaving.

Even though Julianna lived in a flat at the end of Freya and Theo's home in the Blue Mountains now, they were both working through the days and weren't there to take care of her. Their children had long since moved out of home and though they visited often, Julianna had never wanted them to come see her; they would want to take care of her.

"We should get her some flowers," Freya suggested. "Maybe tickets to see that new show in Sydney."

"That's a lovely idea," her mother agreed.

The crackling fire burned orange and red before them, warming the bare skin of Freya's arms. It cast shadows over her mother's wrinkled face and soft white hair.

Freya sipped her homemade chai tea brew, letting the warmth settle deep in her belly.

"I think we deserve a treat tonight," she declared, setting her cup down and heading into the kitchen.

"What kind of treat?" her mother asked, a smile in her voice.

When Freya returned carrying a small tray and two sugary lemon tarts, her mother laughed delightedly.

They sat, as they had for many a year now, sipping a lovely drink and enjoying crumbly citrusy desserts, listening to the crackle and pop of the fire. They were warm and comfortable and well-fed, and enjoying the company of one to whom you have no need to explain yourself, because they have simply been around so long that there are very few parts of you that they don't already recognise.

Freya noticed her mother's gaze stray to the creamy white photo album atop the coffee table. She knew her mother was afraid. Afraid because she did not remember or recognise all the people inside. Afraid because she did not remember herself laughing in those moments. She could not understand what her mother was going through, though she lived with her every day.

"Mum," she began, then paused.

"Yes?"

Freya watched her mother's shaking hands set her mug down on the table.

"What can I do to make all this easier on you?"

She saw her mother stiffen sightly.

They didn't often talk about the dementia. It made her mother sad and uncomfortable, and she claimed that discussing it wouldn't make anyone any better.

Freya didn't really expect her mother to reply, so she was surprised when her mother looked into the fire and spoke softly.

"Moments like these are all I need."

Freya blinked.

"What do you mean?"

Her mother reached a hand into the space between them. Freya, surprised, reached out and clasped her mother's frail, warm fingers. She squeezed gently.

"Just sit with me. And I know that tomorrow, if I'm lucky, I'll wake up and see the mountains and the trees and the birds singing right outside my window. It comforts me knowing that no matter what happens, these moments will be here waiting for me."

Freya blinked back tears. She couldn't think about what would happen if her mother *wasn't* lucky. She focused on the soothing touch of her mother's hand in hers.

Looking back at their lives, she could see that she remembered the little moments they had shared much more than the big things. If someone asked her to retell her life in a story, she would list the big things. Her childhood, her struggles, her relationships, her career, her family and friends. But that wouldn't be wholly accurate, would it?

Because she remembered all those big things through the little moments in which she experienced them. Childhood days were the excitement of her mother buying her the next book in her favourite new series, clutching its smooth sharp cover in her hands. Her struggles were the cold lonely nights with her arms wrapped around her stomach, her lips pressed together to hold back the sobs. Her comforts were Theo's arms around her, strong and warm and steady. Her career was a patchwork – the rush of relief as she submitted a report, the breaking down with stress when she couldn't see her computer screen anymore through her blurry teary gaze, the laughter of her colleagues and friends at the coffee station. She had far too many memories with her mother to remember them all, far too many moments good and bad.

So, she didn't try to remember them all. They sat together and chatted about their morning plans and let the warmth of the fireplace chase away the chill night air.

The Sajdah (prostration)

Naosheyrvaan Nasir

Put your head to the ground
And your back up against the sky
So pour your heart out
There is no judgement
Just you and your Lord

The blood flows through
To your head
Your spirit looking up ahead
At the opportunity that awaits

To the Lord when you surrender
The time that passes is but a number
It feels much like slumber
But in broad daylight the world cut asunder

By thrice reciting "Holy is my Lord the most High"
Your wish list to God can reach for the sky
For it is your moment and yours only
So converse with God all you like

When your head lifts up from the ground
And after finishing your prayer you look around
The world is much the same
But it is you that has changed

Dream Walker

Zara

Bask in the sunshine,
laying on a beach.
Sand whispers through fingers softly.

Run through a forest,
sipping from streams.
Mist-wrapped trees, a sylvan scene.

Cut through the clouds,
wings full of wind.
Make Icarus proud, that gilded beast.

Treading softly,
walk through your dreams.
Wake them up –
to keep you company.

Happy Fifteenth

Carmen Vallis

you hold fast
sit on my lap
though you're my size, my equal
and stop my blood circulating
I am beneath

you laugh
as your eyes and years roll,
I hold too, draw you near
pretend I'm cold
nose-blowing time in tissues

daughter, again and again
we are borne
weathered and caught
in brume and rain
drenching the ground
I have so uncarefully
unprepared for us

phones
the timer goes off
a karaoke of work
scrabbled monopoly
the garden needs weeding
and yet
those seven letters
fifteen

belie infinite characters
as we squeeze, release
blessings and sweets
for no god we believe in
my dear my dear
you are simply more
than I am
we can be
at fifteen.

Things I Find Beautiful

Sarah Nicole Ambrose

The shape of leaves,
the way they glide on the wind.
The delicate softness of feathers,
and the way they feel against my skin.
Rainy days from the comfort of home.
The night sky – unbelievable, and almost magical.
The ocean. In fact, bodies of water in general.
Autumn leaves on the surface of a lake.
Crisp morning air and struggling sun.
A cool breeze.
Sitting in the sunshine,
warm rays on my face.

Stories and storytelling.
Love. Family. Connection.
The minds of children –
so much creativity and imagination.
Old couples holding hands after many years together.
Laughter: the sound,
the feeling, the whole experience.
When humanity defies the odds

and comes together as one
rather than suffering alone. Kindness.

Music, so beautiful it cannot really be explained.
Handwritten letters,
filled with love.
Beautiful art,
filled with passion.
Life –
it's messy, it's hard, but it's beautiful.

Water and Mountains

Hannah Roux

What makes a quick river
come clear? Only one thing
does: water and mountains.

What darts from side to side
like a little fish, hooked
and wriggling? Only one thing:

the country, which you cook
like a small fish, silver,
and steaming. Black coals.

Smoke rises. What untroubles
the troubles? Only one thing
does: water and mountains.

Waters are imprinted
even on emptiness,
the valleys are cupped hands

holding the shape of them.
Cool unclarity, the sharp
kindness of water they hold,

crooked and shining, hooked
on the plunging, fishing
backs of mountains, making

the darkness small and luminous:
violet evenings, flooding
the lacey crowns of mountains.

What makes a quick river
come clear? Only time and
the mountains. Taste the fish

silver and steaming. Winter
bitters the air. Waters
wriggling. Mountain-fingers.

Del o Ghalb

Danny Yazdani

What if I told you that the word "heart" is simply not enough?

What if I said that this meagre term fails to cover the realms of
    existence,
of the real and the fantasy,
of the near and the far,
of what once was and what now is?

Your *Ghalb*.
A beating, living organ
Essential to life.

Your *Del*.
A pulsating, yearning component of the human experience
essential to archiving the experiences of a human.
You.

I am here now, in a far-off land filled with strange creatures and
    exotic foods and
Questionable politics.

My *Ghalb* throbs normally, steadily.
They say that kangaroo meat is good for fighting cholesterol.
But my *Del,* oh, my *Del,* is pushing against my skin from the
    inside.
I can feel it suffocating, gasping for sustenance as it wrestles
    with my organs,
knowing it doesn't belong.

It came first. And it has earnt its place
long before the notion of the *Ghalb,*
before the invasion of a land,
before the conversion of a people,
before the escape of an extended unit,
before the rootlessness of a family tree
clawing at the Earth for stability in an unknown terrain.

The *Del* has warned me of this past,
of the burdens that have seeped through
old bloodlines and will continue to poison
the future generations.

The *Del* has pleaded me to act fast,
to ignore the passivity of the *Ghalb*
whose supposed function is purely to pump blood.

The *Del* has counselled me to hold tightly
to what is held out of my reach,
to taste the bittersweet,
to beckon to its silent screams –

But how can I heed these calls when the *Ghalb*
offers me familiarity,
a comfort in the known,
and a refuge in the borderlands of who I am meant to be?

The Children's Bach

Blake Isaac Falcongreen

For J.E.C.

Your prodigal child now weeps
for the beach at St. Kilda, for her
childhood with coconuts and the
sunscreen that hardly worked, that was
oily and runny. Why was the realm
of pleasure a burning concrete summer?

When the plane trees transplanted
autumn to Melbourne you wandered the
deciduous streets, newfound and corrupted,
and searched for mystery in a stone patchwork,
devoid of the colours of your dreams, bereft
of the wonders behind your strained retinas.

I baulked – you reimagined even
the banality of my bedspread; my own
hands were now different, peculiar, more plain
and exceptional than they had ever seemed.
The child follows you now, with a loyalty
grown by beach palms and glazed in sunburn.

All the Small Things

Djuna Hallsworth

1999

Sitting in front of the CD player.

"Tracks four, five and eight are good." So we only listen to tracks four, five and eight, and skip the rest.

I point at the picture of the person in the fake nurse's outfit with shiny red lips and '90s blue eyeshadow in the CD insert. "Is that a woman or a man? It looks like a woman on the front but this looks like a man here." I examine her hairy-looking arms and broad shoulders, perplexed.

We can't decide, but we know something about it is funny. We get it; we're in on the joke. There's a lot about the album that is funny: the way they say boo-quet instead of boe-quet, the many jarring words I don't know the meaning of but which I know are taboo ("sodomy" sounds odd and rhymes with ADD, sort of), their bemused and sarcastic expressions in the band photos, and how could someone forget their own age? So silly! Over and over and over again. We try to guess which one is Tom, which one is Mark and which one is Travis, based on the photograph of the three of them shirtless in a doctor's office, next to that puzzling, erotic nurse. We eventually find out we guessed wrong.

We try tracks three and six, and seven and nine, sprawled out on the floor of the big room that became mine years later. It has floor-to-ceiling curtains, ornate light fittings and that little extra window in the corner that seems to serve no purpose. It's the only room in the house that has a ceiling fan and I'm envious. Seven is different to the rest, and I know the lyrics from some Nirvana song – they're not the same but similar. From it, I get a foreboding sense of the sadness and despair that adolescence brings. I know that I don't know what it feels like, or how life could be so unbearable; I'm too young. My brother hints that he does, or he might, or maybe he wishes he did. Nine is silly, and we get a kick out of trying to learn the lyrics from the insert and singing along, our tongues tripping over themselves. We debate whether or not she is wearing underwear or whether he just hopes she isn't.

Then it turns out that my friend from the year above me at school likes the same songs. I make a mixtape and take it to her grandparents' house in the hills. We jump on the sofas and shout the lyrics, oblivious to what the words mean. We aren't even sure if we are saying the words right but we feel the . . . what is it? Punk rage? A repressed subversive streak? Dinner is ready, but the song's nearly finished, too.

At some point, my brother and I listen to the whole album. We like track ten best. We call them blink one-eighty-two.

I am seven.

2001

The same bedroom, playing *Donkey Kong* on the Nintendo.

"Listen to this." My brother puts a blank disc into his flashy silver CD player. He calls the song "Holiday". I don't know where it came from – burning CDs is a kind of black magic to me – and it sounds a bit confronting at first; the chorus seems to erupt into a wall of noise, but I begin to like it the more I hear it. He plays a couple of other songs, and they make me picture unruly boys waiting for the last bell and heading to a wild party at someone's huge house. These images are both thrilling and alarming to me; I'm not sure I want to grow up. Teenagers are unpredictable and frightening. My brother knows what they're talking about: the two-dimensional archetypes and the boring cliques. "People at school are just like that. It's so accurate." I smugly agree, but I have no idea.

There are other songs on his mix CD: one from the Pokémon movie soundtrack, some more punk rock and the sound of the era: soft R'n'B. Sometimes aggressive rap, too, but there's only so much of that I can tolerate: the obnoxious refrains stick in my brain and twist and spin until they're muddled up and the lyrics are just sounds. We always have music on when we play *Donkey Kong*. My thumbs hurt from frantically trying to control the movements of the little animated thing on the old television screen, and I worry that I am overdoing it. When I close my eyes to go to sleep at night, I see the fat ape leaping and galloping. I've heard about things like this – about obsessions and addictions – and I don't like the idea of losing control.

We're in the dining room of my mum's friend's house. It's gotten dark and we've ordered pizza. The adults are outside by the pool. "Cover your ears," their teenage daughter tells me. "Yeah," my brother agrees with a smirk. Now I'm too young? At home, we're the same age but when we're out I'm little? Fine, then. I reluctantly put my palms over my ears, but I still catch some things the band say and wish I didn't. They don't sound so good live – not their voices and not the notes they're hitting, or missing, rather. Some of the words they use are crude and I don't think there's any need for it. I decide that I'm not interested in their personal lives, and that I'll push what I've heard from my mind, focusing instead on the music.

I am nine.

2004

There are maybe five or six of us. I feel like a child, and the other girls look like teenagers. My clothes are soft and warm and functional, and theirs are thin and made from fabrics that are synthetic and would snag easily. I feel smaller than them, with a face that's not quite finished and a body that is pink and cold to touch. They wander between each other's houses, not doing anything in particular. I want a plan; I want to know where we're going. I want to go home, but what would be better yet is if they went away and left us alone, the way we used to be. It's hard to fit in when you don't want to. I don't make an effort but even if I did, I don't think it would make any difference.

"What music do you like?" one of them asks.

"Blink-182," I tell her. She seems enthusiastic.

"Oh, I love that song, 'Miss You'," she exclaims. A few others mutter their agreement.

I nod, as if this is predictable. "'I Miss You'," I correct her subtly. "It's my favourite." It turns out it's the only one they know. They don't know "Feeling This" or "Easy Target" or "Always", so we don't have much to talk about. My friend has new friends and so she and I have increasingly less to talk about, it turns out.

Me and her and another girl wander up a steep street. "Guess which house is mine," she demands of me. It's a stupid game and I don't want to play.

"I don't know," I tell her, wishing she'd go away. She's not very nice and I don't think we have anything in common.

"Yeah, but guess."

We keep walking.

"Are you going to guess?"

"Sure."

"So?"

We're almost at the end of the road.

"This one," I say, gesturing vaguely to the house with the front steps and wide lawn.

They are both gobsmacked. "How did you know that?"

I shrug.

My brother has bought the album from JB Hi-Fi and I study the lyrics in the jacket like I always do. There's an atmosphere to songs like "Violence" and "Asthenia" that is absent in the earlier albums. It's harder to drop into, song-by-song, but from start to finish it takes me into myself and not into sun-bleached Southern California. I feel a different kind of yearning: one that's for a space, not a place.

I am twelve.

2011

A corner room with two beds: one by the door and one in the curved nook, beneath the window. My home for three months. I don't feel at home, but it's better than the room across the hall with the rude French girl who smokes and sleeps till 2 pm and skips class and who doesn't like me. The jet lag just doesn't go away, not after a few days or a few weeks. I don't have the energy to pretend. *Isn't it amazing? Isn't it just like Hogwarts? At least we're in Surrey so we'll develop nice British accents, not trashy ones.* I think the Surrey accent sounds whiney and I say so.

My roommate is twenty and that seems old. She visits her boyfriend in a place starting with B – Bromley, maybe? She's there often. We get along okay but we're not friends. I prefer it when I'm alone, except in class or in the dining hall, where being alone makes you painfully visible.

When I go to the Student Union parties, I get ready in my room first, playing music on my laptop. My library grows as I meet people with similar music taste to mine. That's how I end up with *Neighbourhoods*; my uncle's friend gives me a red USB stick with a whole lot of albums loaded onto it. It's a new sound, but one that pulses inside me and shocks me back to life. It wraps me up and whispers – *this is home*. It calls to me as it creeps and slithers down damp, dark tunnels and into concealed spaces. *Come hide with me in here.*

But why is God in there? And children? It's so middle-America-suburban in parts. *That's Tom's influence,* I reflect. *I wish he wouldn't.* Still, it's fresh and alive, something to drink, every day, if I want to. I gravitate towards the poppy, upbeat ones: "After Midnight", "Wishing Well", "Ghosts on the Dancefloor", "Kaleidoscope".

This is their best album. I'll tell people that for years, until I change my mind. No one agrees. Enema of the State *is obviously the best.* Or, sometimes, *it's* Dude Ranch, *for sure.* I can't help but scoff at that.

The countryside stays the same for miles on the other side of the train window, but I stare at it, anyway. I'm outside of myself, my mind blankly registers the golden light spilling through the clouds onto the rolling hills, but my body says nothing at all. I make excuses to stay at my aunt and uncle's house, just a day or two longer. I'm a little more myself away from campus. My MP3 player forces me to listen to the same songs all the time, even when it's set to shuffle – it's cheap – and eventually I'm skipping "Even if She Falls" and "Love is Dangerous" because I've heard them too often.

But "This is Home" pulls me into it and holds me close.

There are no bottle openers and the bottles here aren't screw tops; I never would have thought of that. I knock on someone else's door and they have one. Sometimes, it isn't so bad.

I am nineteen.

2013

A drunken guy – he seems to like me. His friend does, but I'm not interested in his friend. He calls me over to sit with him and talk to him and he's funny. He names some of his favourite things – his favourite bands? I can't remember – and one of them is blink-182. *Oh really?* He's immediately more interesting. He slurs his words. He can get me a ticket to Soundwave. *No, you can't. I checked and they're all sold out.* He promises he can get me one. It's only two or three weeks away. He knows somebody, though. *Okay. If you can get me one, then get me one.* He makes it clear that he's not paying for it.

I've never been to a music festival before. I'm not really interested in the other bands. I want to get a new tattoo ahead of the show – just *blink* in that thick, scrawly font that they use sometimes – but I'm rushing the decision and ultimately decide against it.

It's the afternoon, and hot. Sunny. There's no light show because it's too bright. We made guesses about what they'd open with. Maybe I said "Man Overboard", or "Going Away to College". They open with "Up All Night". But Travis isn't there, and they're so far away, dressed in black: Tom in a long-sleeved top and black jeans, even though it's summer. They don't talk to the audience or, if they do, they don't seem to want to. They seem to not want to be there.

A circle of death breaks out and I'm disturbed by the viciousness of the crowd. Girls on the shoulders of their friends or boyfriends. If they fell, they'd probably die, from the impact or from being trampled on. Part of me thinks it serves them right. I'm too distracted to enjoy the show. I'm small but nobody seems to care about that. I feel unsafe the entire time.

You didn't even know all the words. I'm outraged. *Yes, I did! How would you know, anyway? Were you watching my mouth the whole time? I did!*

I don't remember the set but at least I have a blink-182 singlet and a 2013 Soundwave stubby holder to prove I was there.

I am twenty.

2014

Back in England, but this time I'm grown up and ready. The same friend of my uncle introduces me to the *Dogs Eating Dogs* EP and I feel regret for the time spent not listening to it. I don't like the dogs-eating-dogs metaphor, or analogy, or whatever; I never have, except when my friend used it on her Flight Centre post-holiday survey. "We asked for a swim-up bar. We didn't get one. It's a dog-eat-dog world and honesty is important." I nearly died laughing as we sat on our luggage at Bali Airport, waiting for our delayed Jetstar flight back to Perth.

I hope someone will, one day, sing "Pretty Little Girl" to me, but even if they don't, listening to it is enough. I jog along the sodden footpath and through the forest behind the house, which leads to nowhere in particular and which might as well go on forever: I will never reach the edge because it doesn't exist. It's still "Snakecharmer" and "Natives". They pulse through my bloodstream as I push forward. I turn back before I get lost.

On Christmas Day, we're deathly hungover and it's hilarious and disgusting at the same time. I'm starving but lunch isn't ready until two or three o'clock. I have nothing better to do than to fume over the £150 fine I received for not docking my Barclay's bike properly. They think I didn't park it at all (I did) and I can't afford to lose that much money; on Christmas it is doubly insulting.

Sometimes blink-182 comes on my uncle's playlist at work and it's as if someone has taken up a microphone and is speaking directly to me: I feel proud and self-conscious all at once.

I'm twenty-two.

2016

Before I leave, I load the full album onto my MP3 player – not as individual tracks but as a complete download. I'm still not all that good with digital technology, mostly because it doesn't bother me that I'm not. If I want to skip a song – which I don't, but if I did – I would have to manually fast forward.

I'm apprehensive. It's a calculated gamble but a gamble nonetheless. They could easily – indeed, they almost certainly will – lose fans by proceeding with a new front man, even if it is Matt Skiba. I don't jump on bandwagons and make sure everyone knows that I loved Alkaline Trio long before Matt joined blink-182. "My two favourite bands have combined," I say eagerly. "But it means my standards are set very high!" No one's really that interested in whether or not these standards are met, and I don't blame them; if I were them, I wouldn't care either.

I sit halfway down the bus in one of the single seats. If I don't get through the whole album by the time we reach our next stop, I'll just pick up where I left off next time we climb aboard. The ochre-red desert spans out in every direction. I'm indifferent to most of the other travellers – we get along but we likely won't stay in touch – and I'm happy to plug into the music and imagine my own story unfolding in the grotty Los Angeles of *True Detective 2* or skatepark-date-night-pizza-bar San Diego.

Pulling weeds out of the curved garden strip is fine; I don't mind it. I only wish the green bins didn't fill up so fast. They take a whole week to be emptied and I could get the job done a lot quicker if I had space to dispose of the tall, tough grasses. I regret not taking a "before" photo to which I can compare my "after" shots; I'm impressed by my efforts and I think my hosts will be, too. I have a pretty view across to the Adelaide CBD and all I need to think about is whether there might be spiders or snakes hiding in the overgrown plot.

I write a short post on my phone called *Home is such a lonely place*, and publish it on the travel blog that I have maintained throughout the whole period I lived abroad and which I continue to update as I travel around Australia:

This winter, blink-182 brought out California, *the first album with Matt Skiba. It surpassed all my expectations. It felt alive to me, and sounded like the band I grew up with, but like they'd grown up, too. Not once and for all, but for now. Like me. It sounded like home, but home was different. Sometimes it was lonely, sometimes I was cynical. Sometimes we're out of our minds, and other times we're kings of the weekend. We're sorry, we're not sorry. We're bored to death. We can run, but life won't wait . . .*

I get back from Adelaide in early December and book in to get the tattoo that I want. It's humid in Midland and I'm wary of the people lingering outside the train station. The window's open and the fan is on but it's not enough. "Can we pause a second? It's really hot!" As the needle gets close to the soft part of my inner elbow I breathe deeply and exhale slowly through my nose. It takes longer than the other ones and hurts more: a deteriorating heart with an arrow at the bottom and seven more arrows sticking out of the left side. An homage to my two favourite bands.

My grandma can see my grandpa even when the rest of us can't; I showed her the tattoo at Christmas and she said, "Whatever makes you happy, dear," but now, a few weeks later, she gasps and exclaims, "Oh, look, Alan!" like she's seeing it for the first time. She's exhilarated and she wants to share the moment with my grandpa. I'll never know what he thinks because I can't see him. It's like she's the grandchild, seeing life in new colours, painted with reckless abandon. It's one of the last times I'll see her.

I'm twenty-four.

2019

My parents have rented a small apartment in Kirribilli and there's only really enough space for two of us at the tiny table underneath the window. I play "Blame It on My Youth" on my phone and tell my dad that it's overproduced but still really good. I get anxious around the bridge, because this is where the chorus begins to repeat: where the songwriters and producers get complacent and cycle through the same lyrics, the same melody, just to finish the song off. But he nods and concedes that it sounds good. He asks if they ever write any songs in a minor key and I say "Yes, 'Adam's Song', " but he points out that it's just the guitar and not the vocals. I understand. "Then no."

We go see *Antony and Cleopatra* at the Opera House but I left a pot on the stove and so I text my housemate at intermission. He's out, too, though, and I come home to burnt carrots.

I have to move house soon, at the end of November. It's not good timing. It's a renters' market, everybody says, but you wouldn't know it. I'm always everybody's second choice.

I go back to Perth for Christmas. There's a guy I'm chatting with on a dating app; he says he gets on best with people who listened to blink-182 as kids. His name is Jamie. I tell him I have a blink-182 tattoo and he replies that we'll have plenty to talk about, but the message comes through three times. I laugh it off; it's hardly his fault, but it's a slightly awkward start all the same. *I'm in Perth*, I tell him. *Maybe we can meet when I'm back.* He says that would be nice.

I'm twenty-seven.

2022

It's colder and windier than I was expecting. It's already dark at 4.30 pm, but I pull my hair into two half ponytails and pin my *Happy Birthday* badge to my purple jumper, anyway, determined to have a good time. In the bathrooms, I smear blue eyeshadow onto my eyelids with a crayon, then text Jamie: "What's your ETA?" He doesn't see the message and doesn't reply. I swallow my pride and decide to wait at the big table booked for twenty, but as I come out of the bathrooms, I can see that he's already arrived. "You *are* here!" I'm pleased at the prospect of not having to wait, and drink, alone. "Like, four people will come," I moan. "It's so rainy."

I'm wrong, and the table fills up. I chat to my friends on the left-hand side, then swap places with Jamie so that I can talk to the other people on the right-hand side. We discuss what karaoke songs we're going to sing. "You have to start with a blink-182 song," my friend Rachael insists. "You have to. Which one?"

I browse the list on my phone. "Maybe 'What's My Age Again?' or 'First Date'." She confirms that these are good choices.

Fifteen of us are squeezed into a tight, dark, soundproofed room. I'm dying for a wee but Rachael wants to ask if I want a bottle of champagne. Of course I do. I rush to the toilets because we're already late and I don't want to waste any more of our allocated time.

I choose "What's My Age Again" but there's no lyric track and so I'm tunelessly reciting the words, staring at the screen as if I don't know them off by heart. It sounds terrible, but it's my birthday, and it's karaoke: if there's ever a time and a place to sound terrible, it's now.

No taxi wants to pick us up for such a short trip and we've missed our chance to get the bus. At home, I leave my flowers and presents on the counter and climb into the shower. When Jamie wakes me around 10 am on Sunday morning, I feel weak and nauseous and curse myself for not eating more the night before. We listen to our audiobook on the sofa but I feel sick; I want to cry. He tells me to lie down and rubs my belly until the burning subsides.

"It's all downhill from here," he jokes. It's a refrain that we all use, but none of us really believe it. The hangovers are worse, but I'm still the same person.

"You know what's funny?" I say to Jamie, "'All the Small Things' is by far their most famous song – it's the one that everybody knows – but lyrically and musically it's the least interesting. It doesn't even make any sense!"

"Yeah." He doesn't have much of an opinion, but he listens to mine.

I'm thirty.

Pure Joy

James Puterflam

From where does joy arise and to where does it go?
Abiding in mind's space before elsewhere it flows,
Clouds appear in the sky's ceaseless expanse,
Forming, gathering, and dispersing in dance.

Radiant delight, glowing vibrantly bright,
Warmly embracing body and mind,
Bliss without essence, appearance without form,
Manifest like a rainbow, transient as the moment of dawn.

What of joy devised, developed, contrived,
Does joy differ dependent on cause?
A puddle, rain, a river, the ocean,
All are water, all are wet.

Chasing pleasure, fleeing what's unpleasant,
Marathon athletes, the race is ceaseless,
And if we decide not to race – rest in contentment,
Abiding like space in a fortress of stillness.

Imbued with wealth, the hidden desire of kings,
Fully satiated, needing no more and beholding no thing,
Mighty mountains reside without any movement,
Uttering no speech, an impartial witness,

The simplest of pleasure is without dependence,
Free of contrivance, it is pure and uncorrupted,
Normal, attainable by all, requiring no effort,
Immediate as one's eyelashes, difficult to perceive,
Free, uncontrived, effortless – rest and you'll see.

Rhythm Is Going to Get You

Sharmila Jayasinghe

The moon followed Migara like a balloon tethered to his body. He had his head bent low, not wanting his eyes to see the new moon. "දවිහිමිසිනෙ'සඳ නඹලන'බඳුඩා," his grandfather's voice echoed his soul, a warning to avoid locking eyes with the full moon on a Wednesday so as not to conjure evil omens that portended disaster. Good things were happening in his life again. He wasn't ready to let sightings of the Wednesday full moon take them away. That night was his night. He was hurrying to reclaim a world that he thought he had lost forever. The closer he got to the community centre hall, the more his body became aware of the vibrations, the feet thumping on the ground and the reciting rhythm: "*Theium, Thath, Thath, Theium, Tha.*"

In his enthusiasm, Migara had arrived early. Standing outside the window he watched in silence, not wanting to disturb the performers. An old woman sat on the hard cement with her back erect like a wooden pestle, the long one that is used to pound rice. Her bony hips rested on a cushion for comfort. She had her well-oiled silvery hair pulled back tightly to a bun at the nape of her neck. Cymbals in her hand chimed to the rhythm of her voice: "*Theium, Thath, Thath, Theium, Tha.*"

A troop performed, lined up according to skill. In the front were the best and then the rest. Migara's eyes singled out one, a young woman with dark ebony skin and a somewhat skeletal body, her forehead adorned with a moon-like red dot. He felt kinship with her. Him and her, both dancers through and through. Migara's eyes stayed loyal, never leaving her. The dancer swayed to the crash of the cymbals, a branch in a gentle breeze with no effort, natural like breathing. "*Theium, Thath, Thath, Theium, Tha,*" the old woman chanted. One foot in front of the other, the young dancer walked gracefully, her bosom heaving in anticipation, her eyes shaped like tender leaves searching. Her mudras spoke of the longing of a lover: Ayan longing for Radha.

The maestro sang on the iPod drowning the old teacher's *taalam.*

"*Radha ...*" the singer pleaded in his haunting voice. Migara felt the song in his loins.

"*Look at me with those beautiful eyes.*
Don't hide the mischief on the banks of Yamuna,
Don't hide your face and weep.
I am but human,
I see you,
I never left.
Look at me with those beautiful eyes,
The way you looked at him.
Radha my beloved,

Don't hide the mischief on the banks of Yamuna,
Don't hide your face and weep . . ."

Migara tapped his fingers on the windowsill in time with the gentle movements of her body, humming to the familiar tune. They were enclosed in a singular language only they knew. The vibrations of the footwork, the rhythms floating through the speakers, the tintinnabulation of the tiny cymbals and the recited thalam had no colour, race or creed.

Migara's body felt the beat: *Theium, Thath, Thath, Theium, Tha*. It wasn't the beat of his style of dance, not the *Dhomi, Kitha, Kitha, Dhom* he was used to, but he felt the throb and it breathed life into his soul.

Migara was a fortunate unfortunate. He had been discovered as a dancer when he was just nine years old. His dance teacher had called in on his father's home on a Friday after school. "Captain," the puny man had said, "You know, genius is discovered . . ." He had stammered, dabbing his temple with a large handkerchief and jabbering endless words with no connection.

The unease in the room had grown thicker. Migara's father had cleared his throat. "So, you are saying my son is . . . Spit it out man, tell what you want to say."

The teacher had gone a ghostly white, and spit it out he did, "A dancer, sir. Migara is a brilliant dancer!" Bouncing on the chair, he'd let out a lungful of air, relieved.

Migara's father had gone silent. Presenting a large handkerchief, the likes of what the teacher had, he had wiped his forehead vigorously, a scratch and a wipe.

"Is this true, *putha?*" he had asked finally, eyes searching for the child hidden behind the divan.

Migara had sunk, feeling he had been caught doing something he shouldn't. With hawk-like eyes the young boy had studied his old man: the deep-set eyes weren't burning and turning a bright red like the time he had made aeroplanes with some important official papers; the large hands were not trembling like the time he had catapulted a stone through the living room window. The twitch that appeared on the side of his mouth with anger too was missing. Without surfacing out of hiding, Migara had deduced the absence of those tell-tale signs, which assured him his father wasn't shocked or angry. With the assurance, he had jumped up, presenting himself, and shouted an excited "Yes!"

With his father's blessings, dance had taken charge of Migara's life thereafter. *Dhomi, Kitha, Kitha, Dhom* had become his lullaby. Donning the *Ves* costume, Migara had transformed. He had been like an ancient shaman exorcizing. Migara's body had been in tune with the *gata beraya*. The cymbals obeyed him. It was like he was conducting an opera, his muscles, the beads on his costume, the white cloth tied around his waist, the bells on his ankles, the plates on his shoulders and the silver leaves dangling on his head gear; everything transformed into instruments, musicking, swaying and flexing to his will. He performed the energetic masculine dance with grandeur and grace.

Migara was destined to be a dancer and then he was not.

He had been fitting on a kurti at the tailor shop when a bomb that was targeted for a big-shot politician shook everything around him and took his father's life, his own limb, and ended his dance. "A suicide bomber," they had said, "a woman." Migara was certain he saw the woman moments before she blew herself up. Standing outside on the street, she looked in through the tailor shop window. Migara remembered her. He remembered that indescribable gloom, the hatred and animosity she projected at his father who was standing in his military uniform. No sooner had she left the window than the earth shook and Migara hit the ground. Something large and heavy had crushed the lower part of his body. The agony of it all had caused him to black out. When he finally came to, the world wasn't the same. The woman with the smudged red dot on her forehead had haunted him in his dreams long after that day. Every nightmare culminated in him slithering on the ground like a snake through a field of scattered human limbs escaping the woman, giant in stature, laughing and mocking him.

People around him began to pity him, "Poor invalid. He will never dance again."

The young man floated through like a ship without a captain till his uncle came to his rescue and took him overseas. Migara was nineteen when he unpacked his bags in a foreign country. The change of land didn't necessarily bring changes to his life. At night in his dreams, he still heard the mocking laughter and saw the field of scattered limbs.

During the day he was a wound-up toy, doing what others wanted him to do.

"Bunnings is a good place to work," his uncle had said.

Migara had gone to work at Bunnings.

"TAFE has good courses. Learn a new skill. It will come in handy later," his aunty had said.

Migara had gone to TAFE and followed a course that his aunty perceived would come in handy later.

But it was the words of his friend at work that had given him hope.

"Meena's dance school in Baulkham Hills is looking for a dance teacher. She teaches Bharatha Natyam but is looking for a qualified Kandyan dancer to teach. I recommended you," his friend had said. "Go meet her on Tuesday night. She is expecting you."

Migara wasn't unhappy working at Bunnings, but he had experienced more to life than that. "*Domi Kitha Kitha Dom, Domi Kitha, Kitha dom*" had always been a constant beat in Migara's soul. For a long few years after the attack, his heart refused to beat a "*Domi Kitha*". But the moment his friend mentioned an opportunity to dance again in a place where no one had knowledge of his abilities before he lost his leg, a faint "*Dhomi Kitha*" had begun to beat deep within him, and that night watching the young woman dance, the faint beat had become louder and louder.

Outside the community hall, Migara was dancing once again. His hips crackled like breaking knots off a long sleep. Attaining a perfect *mandiya* with the stump of his leg was difficult but he did it anyway. The foot work wasn't as energetic as it used to be. What his body couldn't, his mind attempted: the whirls, summersaults and jumps. He set his dance free. The pleasure of dancing brought his dead soul to a climax.

A loud crash and a thud woke him from a reality of a dream, his prosthetic had hit the uneven cement and he was in a heap on the floor, upturned plastic chairs scattered all around him. Migara looked for witnesses, struggled to his feet, and let the rhythm consume him once more.

Reflection on a Witching Hour Complexion

Joel Fitzgibbons

Painting the outline of a translucent figure
blurred in the great depths of the darkness.
I require the strangest shade of green, or is it a blue?
Whatever it is, my palette does not hold its hue.

In my life I have never glimpsed such a colour
between mollusk purples and pacific blues.
I resist the urge to say, as I stare at my shoes,
that without it life is duller.

In essence it remains,
in a sense it lingers,

like writing I don't understand
printed on a bottle of a harsh elixir I will never taste.
I refrain from exclaiming: make haste, make haste.
But this is all the time that I can stand to waste.

All pigment fades over time,
yet it is still my conviction
to paint the prettiest picture of them all.

That it will be forgotten in time
is truly of no consequence.

Will it be forgotten in time?

In essence it remains,
in a sense it lingers,

in early hours I sit as an alchemist,
mixing colours both foul and divine
until the concoctions combine.
I shall not call this colour mine.

And why should it belong to me?
It belongs to that hour late at night
when the town has been zapped by cold neon light
and the magics all percolate, looming just out of sight.

In essence it remains,
in a sense it lingers,

but there is no pride held between
a trophy's tawdry gold fingers.
Only paint shall decorate my saint
so that their vibrant stains remain.

About the Authors

Sarah Nicole Ambrose

I graduated from the University of Sydney with a Master of Publishing degree and have worked for several publishers across editorial, marketing, publicity, sales and rights. I worked as an editor on the 2015 Sydney University Student Anthology and was published in a later anthology. As both staff and alumna, I have a great love for USYD. In addition to working for the university, I currently work as a freelance editor and music journalist. When I am not working, I can be found with my nose buried in a good book.

Memi Adams

I am a student at the University of Sydney Business School. I enjoy sketching in my spare time and when I don't have exams, I like to bake delicious cakes!

Caitlin Anderson

I'm currently undertaking a PhD and researching the representation of animals and ecological interdependence in contemporary climate change fiction. I work in a bookstore, I'm a dog person, I like my tea and coffee to be scalding hot, dad jokes are my primary mode of communication, and my favourite books from the past couple of years have been *The Dutch House* (Ann Patchett), *A Gentleman in Moscow* (Amor Towles), *Howards End* (E.M. Forster), and *Bewilderment* (Richard Powers).

Freya Elizabeth Bell

I can usually be found with my nose stuck in a book, whether I am reading or writing. I have been doing both for as long as I can remember. I own far too many books and worry that one day I will meet my fate when one of my bookshelves collapses on top of me. When I am not reading or writing, I enjoy drinking tea, daydreaming, working in my garden and pondering the inner monologue of my cat, Max.

Sophie Bellotti

My multidisciplinary practice explores the interplay of matter and language, and how language carves and becomes material reality in socially and culturally situated ways. Currently working on Gadigal and Wangal land, I am undertaking a Master of Publishing at the University of Sydney, and hold a

Bachelor of Arts (Honours) in Creative Writing and Linguistics from the University of Melbourne.

Zhe Chen (Wooden Peach)

I am just a common female psychology student: love guitar, love folk songs, love singing, once wrote lyrics by myself, a fanatical folk music lover.

Ashleigh Cuthill

I am a mum of three (five if you count the dogs, which I do), a recent Master of Publishing graduate, a wife, sister, daughter and a sometimes writer. I am busy experiencing life and all its pleasures.

Aoife Edwards

I am a student enrolled in the Masters of Publishing at the University of Sydney. I am an aspiring editor and as-of-yet unpublished author. I have been working on my debut novel for years and am anticipating the end of the personal editing stages soon. I have been exploring my love of language since I was a child through avid reading that kept me up till 3 am for many of my teenage years, through writing my own stories since I was eleven, and through studying languages other than English to better understand the beauty and rhythm of words. I loved writing a piece for this year's anthology because to me, being a writer is paying attention to the simple details of everyday life, and the ways those details can reflect abstract and complex ideas. I am grateful for the opportunity to have had a lot of fun exploring my piece and developing my skills.

Tom Evans

I am currently undertaking the Master of Publishing while working full-time in the book publishing industry. I believe a single book has the ability to change someone's life and wish to make books accessible for all. I'd also like to thank the person who got me through this all, the baddest of them all.

Blake Isaac Falcongreen

I am a student, musician and researcher living on Gadigal land. I consider myself a committed autofiction enthusiast.

Joel Fitzgibbons

I was born in Sydney and have been interested in writing for most of my life. When I was six, I commenced writing what I thought would happen in the sequel to DreamWorks's *Madagascar* in prose, and I haven't stopped writing since. To clarify, I've moved on to other projects. The movie came out, and so did I. Now, I'm in my third year of university, looking to explore more substantial writing in the future. Beyond that, I'm in a punk band themed around old electronics, I like green tea with lemon flavouring, and I can never decide on my favourite movie but if you put me on the spot, I'll tell you it's either *Fantastic Mr Fox* or the one I saw most recently. My favourite writers include Sylvia Plath, Kurt Vonnegut, and Chimamanda Ngozie Adichie. I've been previously published in the *ARNA* literary journal.

Djuna Hallsworth

Since completing my PhD in the Department of Gender and Cultural Studies in 2020, I have continued to teach, publish and write: both academic work and fiction. My book *Danish Mothers On-Screen* was published in 2021. I now focus on drafting narrative-based manuscripts from the many notebooks and excerpts I have produced over the years.

Sharmila Jayasinghe

I am a journalist turned author of full-length fiction *Butterfly Kisses* and *The Untold Story of My Lover*. My short stories have been published in *Wordly*, *Verandah* and *Swamp* literary magazines, and in the short story anthology published by the Sinhalese Cultural Forum in NSW. I am a migrant, a wife and a mother. A lifelong learner, I have also been a classical dancer and have lent my voice to radio programs. With a Master's in Creative Writing and Literature from Deakin University, I am currently a PhD candidate at the University of Sydney.

Harold Legaspi

I am a doctoral candidate and an Australian writer. My first book is *Letters in Language* (Flying Islands Pocket Books of Poetry series, 2021).

Charles Liang

I am a final-year economics student and freelance photographer. I am passionate about media, advertising arts and creative direction. Previously, I worked as a commercial photographer for three years and later started to explore fine-art photography and the idea of photography as an expression and language of human/societal formation and development.

Alex Ma (A.E. Leighton)

I am a second-year English major who has always been a purveyor of words. My spare time is spent scattering words on a page, reading or playing the piano.

Juan Pablo Guevara Morales

I was born in Bogota, Colombia on the morning of the 23rd of January 1996. I visited Australia for the first time in 2000 (just after the Olympics in Sydney) and left two years after. I would not come back until 2010, searching for the typical yearnings of any immigrant. Twelve years later, settled in this contradictory yet beautiful country, I have never given up my love for letters and writing. It is perhaps the thing that I enjoy the most in the world and the thing that makes me feel most empowered and at ease. That's me.

Zoe Morris

I am a second-year student studying Politics and International Relations and English. I am interested in writing poetry that illuminates the connections between the environment, memory and the self. I have previously been published in *The Avenue* journal.

Emma Murphy

I am currently completing my Master of Publishing, following a bachelor's degree in English literature and creative writing from UNSW. While I love working through the intricacies of other people's words, I also like to create my own.

Naosheyrvaan Nasir

I am a final year student completing my Bachelor of Arts (Economics) / Bachelor of Advanced Studies (Project Management). My poetry has been published before in *Earth Cries, Diversity* and *ARNA*. My poem stems from my experience as a practising Muslim and its uniqueness in the multicultural and multifaith society that is Australia. I am based in Western Sydney and endure a 1.5-hour commute (one way) to campus. After completing my undergrad studies this year, I look forward to commencing as a graduate in financial services at the Commonwealth Bank. Aside from poetry, I have had letters published in leading Australian newspapers such as *The Sydney Morning Herald, The Australian, The Australian Financial Review* and *The Daily Telegraph*. I have written articles for *The Analyst News* and for *Al Hakam*.

Yasodara Puhule-Gamayalage

I am the daughter of Bhaggya and sister of Yasiru, two human beings for whom words can do no justice. So, I compensate for my lack of poetic prowess with humble artistic flair. The simple pleasures of my life are in fact the greatest of pleasures, and they are the moments I spend with my mother and brother. Wherever they are, is my "Home".

James Puterflam

I am a PhD Student in the Faculty of Medicine and Health researching sleep in people with low back pain. I developed my passion for writing through the thesis I wrote during my Honours research year in 2020. As a writer, my focus is the mind, which I attempt to describe in appearance and function inspirated by the words of Buddhist masters and by reflecting on my own day-to-day experience. I appreciate that while we can "share" experiences with others, they are in fact personal and unique. Nonetheless, my expression through poems is an attempt to share such experiences. Beyond writing, I enjoy teaching anatomy with the department of anatomy and histology at the University of Sydney. I spend time meditating, being active, cooking, riding my motorcycle and hanging out with my cat Memphis.

Yusur Razaqe

I am a clay artist of oddly shaped teapots (prone to cracking in the furnace) turned painter turned drawer/doodler. Practising playing the piano until I no longer feel the desperate urge to whiteboard-mark the keys with their respective letters. Painting what I can't put into words. Binge reading until I'm familiar with tsundoku. Gardening so that the floral scent eventually overcomes the petrichor. Lighting enough candles until my room is an aromatic candle haven. When overwhelmed by the disaster that sometimes tends to come with reality, I turn to simple pleasures like these until a sense of hygge embraces me. And even then, I continue to relish those simple pleasures, my sources of sweet euphoria.

Diana Reid

I am a Sydney-based author and University of Sydney alumna. My debut novel, *Love & Virtue*, was an Australian bestseller and won several prizes, including the ABIA Book of the Year Award and the *Sydney Morning Herald*'s Best Young Australian Novelist Award. My second novel, *Seeing Other People*, was released in October 2022. I have also written opinion, criticism and essays for several publications including

Vogue Australia, *The Australian*, *The Sydney Morning Herald* and *The Good Weekend*.

Hannah Roux

I am a PhD candidate in the Discipline of English, a writer of poetry and creative non-fiction, and a dispenser of lectures to those unfortunates who show an interest in what I happen to be working on. My creative work has been published in *ARNA, 1978* and the University of Sydney student anthology, and by the magazine *Insights*. I live and work in Sydney, where I am currently owned by an aging Border Collie named Lucky.

Lindsay Rui

I am a media student and freelance photographer. On the path to becoming a professional communicator, I have a passion to explore a wide range of communication tools of writing, photo, video and emerging technologies.

Atticus Santamaria

I am a creative who has been developing my skills in writing for the past decade and is beginning to offer my work to the public. With many stories, short and long, I look forward to sharing them with readers.

Nicholas J.J. Smith

I am a philosopher, photographer and musician based in Sydney.

Susanna Smith

I am a Sydney-based writer and communications professional who graduated from the University of Sydney with a Master of Media Practice (with Merit). My travel and feature stories have been published in *The Australian*, *International Traveller*, *Wellbeing*, *Culture Trip*, and the *Sydney Morning Herald*. I am currently studying Creative Writing at the University of Technology Sydney.

Carmen Vallis

I am a writer and educator living on Djarrawunang land and working at the University of Sydney. I hold a Master of Creative Writing, a Master of Education and am a PhD candidate in Creative Writing at the University of Notre Dame. I also blog, write educational articles, and am an Associate Editor for an academic journal.

Vanessa Vu

I am currently studying psychology at the University of Sydney, hoping to become a contributor to science communication or journalism. In my free time, I like to flit between hobbies I haphazardly pick up. Previous endeavours include building a crystal radio, recording, editing and mixing audio narrations, and knitting. Despite this, writing has always been a stable part of my life, and I don't think it will leave any time soon. At least, I hope it won't.

Tom Williamson

I'm a mechatronics engineering and arts student at USYD. I am very passionate about fantasy and sci-fi fiction. I love using opportunities such as these to improve my fantasy work. I love exploring different magic systems and the way that it might shape someone who lives in that world's life.

Danny Yazdani

I am an English and Sociology student. I write in my spare time or, more importantly, when I am struck by an overwhelming feeling or sensation that I can only express to others through the written word. I hope to bring justice to the world one day, whether that be through the practice of social work or through literary means. However, if opportunity strikes, I hope to be a multimodal writer across the literary, poetic, and theatrical fields. As a member of the Iranian-Australian diaspora, I am fascinated by topics of biculturalism, masculinity, intergenerational trauma and theatre. My favourite quote is, "Hope will never be silent".

Zara

I am an avid reader and aspiring writer.

Cecile Zhang

I am a self-taught artist based in Sydney, Australia. Born and raised in Shanghai, China, I moved to Australia to pursue my passions for art and life. Working and practising in graphic design and media areas led me to a love of the craft, resulting in a contemporary take on the much-loved combination of different techniques.

About the Editors

Freya Elizabeth Bell

My childhood was somewhat nomadic and stories were always my constant friends. I knew, from a young age, that I wanted to tell and share stories and encourage the love of storytelling that I have always known. As I am now pursuing a career within the book industry, I am grateful that I am able to fulfil my childhood dreams. I'm an avid reader whose TBR never seems to shrink and an incorrigible tea drinker. When I am not reading or writing, I can usually be found daydreaming or watching *The Lord of the Rings* for the hundredth time.

Sophie Bellotti

I'm new to Sydney, currently writing, working and studying on Gadigal and Wangal land, having recently moved from Melbourne. I came to study publishing via my own poetry practice and my general love for language as a creative medium. Sharing in someone's creative process is always a privilege, and being a part of the anthology has been a wonderful opportunity to work alongside fellow writers and artists.

Rose Cousins

Reading is the perpetual hobby that fills the spaces in my schedule. Whether I read high fantasy, trashy romance or non-fiction, or sometimes take a few-months-long break from the habit, it endures. Books and stories abound, filling my home, my thoughts, and my time. And now, I am lucky enough to be studying publishing at the University of Sydney, where I am learning to create and collaborate, to nurture new books into existence. I am thrilled to be working on the 2022 Anthology and can't wait to see all our hard work come to life!

Kiya Elphick

I've never been good at talking about myself so that's why I fell in love with reading and writing stories. This long-time love began in the walls of my primary school in Campbelltown, it took me to Canberra where I became a published writer and decided a career surrounded by books was my dream, and that's how I ended up here at USYD in the last semester of my Masters of Publishing, working with this wonderful team of creatives at the University of Sydney Anthology. I can't wait to see where the magic of words takes me next!

Michaela Gall

I have always loved the magic of creating and sharing stories, and so it makes sense that this is where I've ended up! I made the move from Perth to Sydney to study publishing at USYD with my bookshop experience in one hand and my love for stories in the other, and recently secured a role at Scholastic Australia. When I'm not working or studying, I'm desperately trying to chip away at my ever-growing TBR shelf or ranting to my friends about which author I feel personally attacked by that week!

Natalie Moussa

Being a consumer of all kinds of stories has always been a big part of my life, but reading books shaped me into the person I am today – I've lived many lives through them. English isn't my first language but that just means I have double the amount of books in my TBR. I'm currently halfway through my Master of Publishing and would love to work in the industry. When I'm not working or studying, you can find me baking the latest cheesecake recipe I found (still in search for the perfect one), listening to Taylor Swift (*Taylor's Version*), or rereading *Percy Jackson* for the millionth time.

Vijeta Prasad

I've always been a lover and a collector of stories, and books in particular have hooked me since day one. So, it's only natural that I'm studying the Master of Publishing, and continually seeing books in a different perspective. I'm hoping to be an editor someday (whenever you're ready, Penguin). I'm also pretty fond of cooking, crochet and my cats – what I call the good life.

Lucie Thompson

I've loved working on the anthology for the past two years and I can't wait for you, our readers, to experience the wonderful talent of the USYD community. Books have been a constant source of inspiration, escapism and companionship for me since I was a child. In between working and studying, I'm usually found browsing through the aisles of a bookshop or three and adding to my increasingly overloaded TBR pile.

Kelly Ung

I've been an avid reader all my life and have loved jumping into stories. After having worked at many bookstores and constantly reading, it only made sense for me to pursue a Master of Publishing and a career in books. When I am not studying or working, I can be found with a mug of tea and whatever three books I'm currently reading. It has been a privilege to have worked on *Moments in Between* and *Networks* (Sydney University Anthology 2022) with the incredible contributors of the USYD community.